A BILLIONAIRE WITH BENE...

LENA SKYE

Fancy A FREE BWWM Romance Book??

Join the "**Romance Recommended**" Mailing list today and gain access to an exclusive **FREE** classic BWWM Romance book along with many others more to come. You will also be kept up to date on the best book deals in the future on the hottest new BWWM Romances.

* Get FREE Romance Books For Your Kindle & Other Cool giveaways

* Discover Exclusive Deals & Discounts Before Anyone Else!

* Be The FIRST To Know about Hot New Releases From Your Favorite Authors

Click The Link Below To Access This Now!

Oh Yes! Sign Me Up To Romance Recommended For FREE!

Already subscribed?
OK, Read On!

Summary

"Don't call me unless I call you.

Don't tell your friends about me.

And definitely do not tag me on social media."

These were some of the rules that barista Mikaela Johnson had to live by whilst she was dating Billionaire Justin Henderson.

Justin did not want anything serious. Just a friends-with-benefits relationship and nothing more.

And in this case the benefits were too good to turn down.

Rent paid for. Fancy gifts. Fine dining. Exotic vacations. And the company of a desirable man. Not many girls could say no to that.

It was a good life to have but very soon Mikaela was to discover that everything she ever believed about her billionaire with benefits was not as it originally seemed...

Contents

Chapter 1

She had that beguiling, wide smile that many loved to see. One would expect to see that kind of smile grace the covers of magazines, billboards, and maybe on those pesky YouTube ads. That smile couldn't be found there, however. Her smile was constantly found in a coffee shop, at Uncommon Grounds, a home-grown brand that had given her a job for the last year and a half.

Mikaela Johnson enjoyed her work as a barista and had been recently promoted as shift supervisor. She didn't want to take it, she knew she wouldn't be working there forever, but upon the insistence of the octogenarian owner himself, she relented.

The spunky twenty-four-year-old had bright, hazel-colored eyes, as well as her trademark grin. On her nose was a smattering of freckles which was pleasantly surprising against her umber-toned skin. Her black hair came in thick waves that hung on her shoulders, suiting her heart shaped face. She preferred this to long hair, and it didn't look too tomboyish either. Just a good wash and wear for her work schedule.

The day began like any other day, a day she had been used to. Mikaela loved the smell of coffee, but she wasn't a heavy drinker. She made excellent drip coffee, though, which was one of the reasons why Uncommon Grounds didn't want to let her go.

She was glad that they didn't. It meant she was valued and loved by her peers and bosses. It was important for her to be respected. She had worked honestly and judiciously and was pleased her efforts had worked. If her parents were still alive right then, they would have been proud. Mikaela thought about the other goals she hadn't achieved yet. She was going to get there someday; she wasn't quite sure when, but someday. It was a promise she made to herself and a promise she made in front of her parents' graves. Morbid as it seemed, it was a source of motivation. There was nowhere else to go but up, right?

While the owner of Uncommon Grounds didn't want her to be just an ordinary barista, his patrons still wanted to see the bright young woman serve their coffee. If they couldn't remember her name, they remembered her grin, which was good enough for Mikaela. To the keen observer, she wasn't extraordinarily pretty, but her features were well proportioned, except for that mouth that loved to turn up at the corners. When she smiled, her existing looks magnified even more, rendering her at her most attractive.

"Don't you want to be a model?" a patron asked her today.

She shook her head as she received his card to swipe.

"I don't think that's going to work for me. I'd like to be in the medical industry."

"Yeah, you'd cure people with that personality of yours," the elderly gentleman said as she handed him his card and receipt.

"I'mma just serve it to you, all right?" she told him. She liked Mr. Jordan. He was a former NASA technician and lived in a nearby retirement home, but was ambulatory and enjoyed taking walks along the beach which was just a few blocks down the street. Uncommon Grounds had fascinating patrons in the two years she had worked here.

She had moved from Washington a few years ago after the deaths of her family members. Mikaela had hoped for a fresh start after enduring difficulties in the wake of their passing. It was a slow, painful process and one of those rare times that she found it difficult to smile.

Getting hired in a fast-food joint was just the start as a nineteen-year-old living all alone in California. It was where she'd met one of her closest friends, Lynne Young. Fast forward years later, she was working in a coffee shop and Lynne had become an account agent for a global bank.

Lynne had wanted her to work in a bank, but she enjoyed the aura in the coffee shop. The pay wasn't amazing, but it was decent and it gave her time to teach kids dance at a local studio on weekends. She wasn't paid for that, but she counted it as a sort of giving back to the community labor.

"Hi." She gave her trademark bright smile, facing a customer. "Welcome to Uncommon Grounds; what'll you be having for today?"

He was someone she hadn't seen yet. A new face. He was a nonchalant-looking man, wearing a charcoal gray suit and sunglasses. He scanned the menu board and she quickly gave him a copy on the counter.

"Here, to make things easier," she said, pushing the menu in front of him.

"I like making things difficult," he said in a quiet voice. He had a wonderful inflection, she realized. There was a moment of silence. "I'll have the caramel macchiato with low fat milk. Easy on the caramel drizzle."

Mikaela wondered what he meant by what he said, but she nodded anyway, ringing the order up. "Can I have your name? Would you like a membership card? Points get you free stuff," she said.

He shook his head and paid for it in cash. "Justin."

"I'll call your name in a few."

He said nothing and proceeded to an empty chair. He sat down and faced the window, patiently waiting for his order as he diddled on his phone. Mikaela thought he wasn't the friendly type and he probably wasn't from this side of town either.

"Drink for Justin," she called out moments later.

The tall, brooding-looking customer came up to the counter, said a quick thanks, and left a hundred-dollar tip after taking his first sip of

Uncommon Grounds' caramel macchiato. They made their caramel drizzle from scratch, and it was one of their most popular drinks.

Her eyes widened, seeing the bill on their communal tip box.

"Did you see that?" her co-worker, a trainee named Kimberly, asked, clearly amazed. "He left a hundred. A hundred buck tip for coffee that only cost him three fifty."

"Good: you're starting to recognize the prices for our products," Mikaela told her.

"Are people always that generous here?" Kimberly said, still awed.

Mikaela shrugged a bit. "He was a weird one. And he must've really liked his first sip. Hooray for Uncommon Grounds."

Her ten-hour shift was a breeze. It was past five in the afternoon when her work hours finally ended. Her phone rang just as she had taken off her apron.

"Where are you?" that familiar, high pitched, yet comforting voice asked her.

"Work. Well, it just ended," Mikaela told Lynne.

"Listen," Lynne began, "so there's this party this weekend. It's a cocktail event—"

"And you need to borrow a dress?" Mikaela teased.

"Sadly, no. I got a new one, because this is an investor's event. Okay, where was I? I need a date."

This surprised Mikaela. Lynne almost always had a date wherever she went. The blonde bombshell was a hit with men with her honeyed voice and Southern accent. She and Lynne were opposites in many ways, but managed to become very close.

"You need a date?" Mikaela laughed. "Why don't you get one from the party?"

"I need the cheerleader effect," Lynne said earnestly. "There'll be a lot of men there, and it's a manly world, after all."

"Don't you have friends from the bank? Or the banks?"

"I need someone they don't know."

"Ouch. I just might get popular someday."

"As the world's number one barista?" Lynne teased. "Or as America's best nurse?"

"Har har."

"Come on, Mikaela. Saturday will be your break day, right? I need to show you off, too. It'd be unfair if they only saw me. We're both single and ready to mingle with the big shots."

"Are you husband hunting?"

"Just potential dates. They're sure to have money. Or if they have significant debts, I'm sure they have other assets."

"Oh my God, you're starting to think like them," Mikaela said in mock horror.

"I'm thinking for my future," Lynne corrected. "So what do you say?"

"Well… Lynnie, I have dance classes."

"Oh psshh. They'll be fine without you for that day. Besides, you're not even getting paid for it."

"I don't mind not getting paid, Lynne. You know it's—"

"Giving back to the community," Lynne interrupted with a sigh.

"Come on, be a dear to me, will you? I haven't seen you in two weeks and a few hours is all I'm asking for. Would it kill you to look prettier than you usually are for a night? In heels and a nice dress?"

"Now it sounds like you really want to borrow a dress," Mikaela laughed.

"Actually I thought about that little number you bought the last time we went shopping. The gold A-line dress?"

"Knew it."

"I'm so glad we're the same size. So I'll pick you up this Saturday, six o'clock sharp?"

Mikaela huffed. "Fine. How fancy is this party anyway that you have to dress like you're gold bullion or something?"

"Just a lot of big wigs I'd like to impress. You might catch someone big too," she joked.

"You and your double entendre shit," Mikaela said.

"Oh you're using fancy words aren't you?"

Mikaela laughed. "I read about it, researched a bit about it. I'd like to use big words every now and then that I don't understand to make—"

"Myself sound more photosynthesis," they finished together and laughed.

"I'll see you Saturday, all right?" Lynne said in her trademark croon.

"All right. See you. Love ya."

"Love ya, too."

The other line clicked. Mikaela put her phone down to stretch a little. Her neck ached and she massaged it a bit. Then she grabbed her bag to head out to the parking lot. The sun was sinking over the horizon and it had been a long day. She thought about what to cook for that night. Something easy. Or she could cook nothing and just sleep and starve her way to a diet.

Mikaela was a thin woman, and Lynne teased her about her boobs and her butt. "Those are so not a black woman's assets," she'd tease her good naturedly.

Lynne was the only one who could tease her that way, and Mikaela teased Lynne in the same harsh, yet comical manner. Mikaela drove down the street, feeling the cool air come from the ocean. She loved the beach, but had seldom gone to one in months. Life just happened, working life just took over her.

She drove a beat-up car, a 2005 Honda Accord she had paid for in cash. She loved the car nonetheless, despite its aging exterior and interior. Lynne had joked she could sell it as an antique. She didn't want to, for practical, monetary purposes. She had saved a substantial amount, enough for two years of nursing school, but that was only two years, far from the bachelor's degree she wanted. She'd have to work three more years at the café or find work that paid at least $4,000 a month. Or she could leave the apartment she had come to love. It was a studio, twenty-four square meters of neatness that she tried to decorate well enough, like the ones in architectural digests. She bought used furniture, salvaged abandoned pieces and did those DIY projects that she had come to hate and love at the same time.

She tried to incorporate bits and pieces of her childhood into her apartment, whatever she remembered was in their old house, that old house with its picket fence and the tall columns. Her father had been the only child, and her mother was also an only child. Mikaela and her brother had a happy childhood and she had been spared from that accident only because she played hooky.

They were attending her brother's awarding of Best in Reading and Best in Math for his grade year. She was fifteen years old and had gone through that rebellious stage where she wanted to hang out with her friends and get to know a few boys better, perhaps score a date. She had used the excuse that she needed to do some group study.

She had regretted that moment in the deepest parts of her soul. She could have died with them, but she was alive because she lied. To give some semblance of comfort to herself, she felt that she was alive for a purpose. Her whole family had left her on earth for a purpose. She didn't want to delve in the pain of it, so she forced herself to move forward to the best of her youthful ability.

There were times that Mikaela felt lonely, but she didn't let it get the best of her. In the rarest times, on one of those cold nights in Malibu, she would walk down the beach and listen to the sea just to alleviate her loneliness and the memory of her family.

***

The nonchalant-looking man, wearing a charcoal gray suit and sunglasses, walked out of the café after taking a few sips of his coffee. It was good coffee, he had to admit, and he'd had coffee in five-star hotels in far flung mountains during his travels and in the comforts of his own homes. Plus, the barista had this lovely smile he wished was on some of his employees' faces. He was happy to give that hundred-dollar tip; it would brighten the minimum wage people's days for sure.

Justin Henderson was a twenty-eight-year-old businessman with a knack for making millions in hours. His muscular build and his strict mouth certainly helped with business, as everyone took him seriously. Physically he wasn't intimidating, although he was a force that no one would have wanted to reckon with. His dark eyes made people conscious, and those who were supposedly confident in their tasks were no longer sure if it was done properly—all for the way he stared.

He also had a beard that he maintained at a maximum length, which was a hassle, but it made him recognizable as Justin Henderson, businessman extraordinaire. Justin Henderson wore tailor made suits and genuine leather shoes made by artisans in Italy. He was rather vain and justifiably so. One had to look the part of the successful, powerful man who didn't have time to look the least bit sloppy.

This was why he avoided the beach even though he loved it; e the beach made him look too casual, which he didn't like the world to see. While he wasn't paparazzi material, there were still media hounds that liked to follow him around. He dated popular women after all, from celebrities to models and daughters of millionaires.

He was glad that they stayed away from his immediate family, and he was glad they were in England, far from the madding crowd who liked to milk everything, from what whichever actress wore, to who did whom.

The only son of a steel magnate and a baroness, Justin helmed his father's conglomerate as soon as he graduated college, a difficult feat, but one he managed with aplomb that was unheard of in his age. His father had died three years ago, and his source of strength and infinite wisdom had been relegated to him and him alone.

He had two younger sisters, both still in finishing school. His mother was busy with charity work, something she loved doing better than office work. The hours and the meetings stressed her out, so she opted from the company and only represented the charity/foundation and was a consultant for their socio-civic duties.

In England as a student, the media hounded him. They were fascinated by him, popular not by choice, but by public demand. He had thought that moving to America would improve his chances of living a normal life. He was wrong. The European media followed him soon after, much to his chagrin.

Justin liked to keep his private life as private as possible, but the women he dated wanted otherwise, loving their time in the tabloids and social media sites. He scoffed at the headlines he had seen often about his dating life.

Billionaire to Propose to Model Girlfriend.

Justin 'Hunky' Henderson Seen Canoodling with (insert name of A-list actress here).

Is it Over? Justin and Jessica Call it Quits.

Ah, Jessica Kendrick. He was crazy for her for a few weeks. With that hot body and vibrant personality, who wouldn't be? Then that lovely feeling of being in love dissipated quickly. It was always like that. But they did date for quite a while. A year and a half to be exact. It was an ugly breakup, one she still carried a grudge for and he didn't blame her much, except that she had thought he would propose.

Silly girl. He dated another, and then another in quick succession. There was no shortage of women for him. Of course, Jessica would rear her beautiful head out once in a while to wreak havoc and stay in the news. That was the problem with beautiful, hot-headed women. They were as crazy as they were beautiful. It was proportional.

"Sir, we have a little bit of trouble," his secretary rang.

Jesus, what the hell was this now? "What's going on, Lori?" he asked.

"She's here." It was simply said, but Justin already knew what it was about. Just when he thought things had gone smoothly, she just had to be here on such a fine morning.

"Why does she know I'm here?" he said irritably.

"Her stalking skills have improved as of late," his middle-aged secretary remarked.

"Jesus," he muttered.

He didn't have the time to face this, more importantly, he didn't have the right attitude to face this. He wanted himself mentally prepared (also just a bit physically if she ever intended to slap him), for the onslaught of her feminine wiles, which drove him to the brink of gritting his teeth in frustration.

"Shall I let her in before she causes a scene?"

"And then let security escort her out?" Justin sighed. "Fine. Show her in."

He only had to take three full breaths before she barged in and shut the door behind her with a bang.

"You know, that door is mahogany," he remarked. "What can I help you with, Jessica?"

She was a pretty angry little thing and he suddenly wanted to comically draw over her face, maybe add some steam on top of her head and claws on her fingers.

"We've only broken up for six months and now you're parading yourself on the news?" she huffed.

"Doing what? My job?"

"No! You're dating a fellow model! Someone I personally know! What the hell is wrong with you? Have you no shame?"

"Wait, who the hell are we talking about?" he said with amusement.

"Caitlyn Collins!" she snapped, grabbing something from her designer bag. Justin heard keys jangling and other items being moved about inside her large bag.

She whipped out a tabloid and slammed it on his table. "There!" She pointed with a well-manicured finger. Her finger landed on one picture, one of three, where Justin and Caitlyn were strolling around the streets of New York while eating gelato in sugar cones.

Ah, Justin remembered, this was two weeks ago. It had been an all right date, but they ended their arrangements amicably, citing their busy schedules. Caitlyn was definitely nicer than Jessica, except sometimes it felt like her head was floating on the clouds, or maybe she was high on marijuana. Whatever it was, it didn't work out and Justin quickly put it behind him.

"What's it to you?" Justin said. "She's a nice person."

"But I'm not," Jessica snapped.

"I think that's why I broke up with you," Justine said good-naturedly.

Her eyes widened and her jaw clenched. "No one breaks up with me—"

"I already did. Six months ago. Did you suffer from short term memory loss or something?"

She wanted to scream, he knew it. She wanted to be the diva that everyone knew she was. Jessica Kendrick had a vicious temper, but fashion houses still hired her, and events wanted her because she had a gorgeous face, that, unfortunately, he no longer found appealing.

To him, she was just another pretty face in the crowd and he could date just about anyone that had a pretty face. He was Justin Henderson, anyway. Not that he had an ego. He had a huge ego. His position did that to him.

Jessica's face was red; she was thinking of something vicious to say. She had a sharp tongue, which was one of the reasons why he broke up with her. He had a few solid reasons. But the best one was that she was bat-shit crazy.

He smiled at her. "Shall I have a car bring you somewhere?"

"You think you're the best thing that's happened to me, right?" Jessica began. "You think you're the greatest person to walk the face of the earth?"

"You and I only dated because we both have huge egos and we thought we'd be suitable for each other," Justin told her matter-of-factly. "Did you just come here to show photos of me dating your friend?"

"She is *not* my friend," she seethed. "You're doing this on purpose, dating people I know, and dating other models."

"There is no law against that, last I heard."

"You're doing this on purpose," Jessica insisted.

"So what if I am?" he responded. "I'm a single man enjoying his single life. I see no crime with making anyone feel bad just because I think they deserve it."

"You think I deserve it?" she gasped.

He nodded, unfeeling. "Of course I do. You're a little pocket of bitchiness and I didn't want any more of it."

"I loved you."

"I did too, but things change. Like how I feel for you, which actually borders on derision."

She was shaking her head, on the verge of tears, but she wouldn't give him the satisfaction that he had won. He was an asshole, she had known this the moment she dated him, but he was a fun asshole, and he was well oiled. She had gone three months without significant income a year ago and he didn't question her independence. He provided her with everything she wanted and needed, even paid for her rent until the industry found something for her again.

She didn't want to lose that source of assurance in her life. He really was generous and that was what she missed about their relationship. And the sex, my god the sex. He was tireless and she hadn't found anyone that could match his libido, even if she did not lack in men who were interested in her and what was in between her thighs.

She spun around, unable to say anything, the harshness of Justin Henderson had stung her again. She would not cry in front of him, she would not. So she took a deep breath, gave a smile that bordered on psychotic 1950s housewife and walked away.

"Do you need a car?" he asked her.

She paused and took another deep breath, her hand on the door. "No," she replied refusing to look at him.

Justin said nothing more and watched her walk out again, the second time she had done that in the six months that they had broken up. He had a feeling it wouldn't be the last time he would see her. He couldn't even talk to his mother or sisters because Jessica would get jealous over the attention he gave them.

He would continue dating others, people she probably knew, and that would cause her to spiral out of control again and act like the woman that she was and always will be. Some sadistic part of him surfaced; he had wanted to see her cry. She had given him enough stress and he thought he deserved to make her cry, no matter how childish it seemed. She had never cried in front of him. He only loved a few women in his life and that included the women in his immediate family.

He shrugged to himself and went back to his desk, knowing the day was going to be much better.

Chapter 2

"And I am on my way," Lynne told her over the phone. "Sorry, I'm running a little bit late."

"Weren't you supposed to borrow my dress?" Mikaela asked, laughing. "You've got forty minutes before your event starts."

"It isn't my event, but I wish it was. Catch you later. Bye."

The receiver clicked and Mikaela chuckled as she put her phone down. She had estimated that Lynne was going to be here in ten, dress in ten, and take selfies for another ten. That girl loved her selfies.

She bolted up from her loveseat and walked for her closet. She flung it open and took out the dress Lynne was going to borrow. Now what she going to wear? She picked out a cobalt blue number, a figure-hugging dress with a hint of cleavage in the middle of it. She had the perfect shoes for it. Mikaela disliked stilettos and if she could, she preferred to be barefoot or in sneakers.

"You don't wear sneakers or flip-flops if you want to move on top," Lynne would tell her.

She would tell Lynne she had no plans of being in the corporate world or the fashion industry where stilettos were needed and Lynne would "tsk" at her and express to Mikaela she'd need some in the near future. "Who knows," Lynne said, "you just might date someone who's past six feet."

She promised to herself she wouldn't date anyone who was exceedingly tall, citing it would be difficult to get romantic kisses and hugs and it would look awkward in pictures. Her ex-boyfriends were five-foot-nine at most. She hadn't dated in over a year, much to Lynne's disappointment. She wondered if this was why Lynne wanted her to be her date for tonight's event, so she could set her up with some corporate man.

Sure, set me up with a billionaire or something, she scoffed as she put her dress on, *because everyone billionaire will have eyes for me, right?* Lynne could get a millionaire if she wanted to, and she was sure Lynne could get a billionaire if millionaires weren't available.

She had done her makeup earlier, hoping it still looked all right. The air was rather humid tonight and she didn't want to look like a train wreck by the time she and Lynne got to the party. She was in good spirits when time Lynne rang on her doorbell, with thirty minutes to spare. Lynne quickly changed into the dress she fancied, admiring herself on Mikaela's only full-length mirror.

"Could you scoot a little?" Lynne asked her so she could appreciate her outfit more.

Mikaela huffed then smiled. "Yeah, yeah, your curves are perfect in all the right places."

Lynne stuck out her tongue. "I know, right?"

"Think that's gonna snag a few men?"

"Boys, men, whatever, as long as they got what I want," Lynne said with a laugh. "And I kind of want a lot, I tell you."

Mikaela shook her head and chuckled. "Damn it, Lynne, you'd better be careful. Some of them might be married."

"I know who is and who isn't in the office, so I'm careful there. Tonight's a different thing, that's why I want to look like a million bucks, all glittery."

"Is there even some dress code to this? For all we know it'll call for those fancy shmancy full length dresses, or maybe ankle length skirts with shawls."

Lynne scoffed. "All it said was cocktail. It's like half a party and half a corporate event or something."

Mikaela smiled. Lynne had a way for explaining things in a funny and vague manner, one that she still understood. There was a reason why they were friends.

"Oh damn it, I was so busy oohing and aahing over myself that I missed out on your look for the night. Give it a twirl?" Lynne asked her, focusing on Mikaela this time.

Mikaela gave an awkward twirl and Lynne laughed at it. "Oh, you're looking fabulous all right in those bedroom slippers. I hope you still have those heels. Remember that impulse buy?"

"Oh those heels that you forced me to buy?" Mikaela's face looked sour.

"Yes, those. Those were beautiful. I suggest you wear them!"

"You mean insist?"

"Whatever, they're both the same. Come on, hurry up, there's still like a fifteen-minute drive to the hotel."

"I was waiting for you," Mikaela said.

"Well come on!"

Mikaela drove a newer Honda, and she told Mikaela to replace her antique one, telling her it wasn't fitting. Mikaela scoffed at the idea, it was impractical and expensive. Besides, she was on a barista's wage. She rarely went shopping with Lynne and on those rare occasions, her buys were ridden with guilt or doubt, even the mere buying of shoes.

The ride was smooth, until they got to the hotel. Valet parking had a line and suddenly, Mikaela was glad that she was riding in Lynne's car and not her own. She saw the cars ahead of them, all branded cars, cars whose names she couldn't pronounce. Unexpectedly, she felt nervous. She realized she hadn't been to any formal events in years, the last one was prom, in the school gym and a good friend had lent her a dress to wear. It was a night filled with awkward and forgettable events, she had had her first sloppy kiss there, too.

She and Lynne got out of the car and walked up to the hotel, with Lynne morphing into a social butterfly. So many "hellos" and "this is my friend Mikaela." She had lost track of the names and faces that had been introduced to her, some even looked like her customers at the coffee shop. Or were they?

"Let me just talk to this person over there," Lynne whispered to Mikaela, referring to a middle-aged couple a few feet away from them.

"Why? Who are they?"

"It's who is he. That old geezer is a horny bastard and he's been sending signals. Don't worry, I won't sleep with him," Lynne joked. "I just need him to invest. Then, hello promotion and suite with a window and a couch."

Mikaela watched as Lynne sauntered her way through the crowd, enjoying the stares by the men and the room, and the stares of envious or annoyed women. She smiled to herself, wondering if she would ever be that confident. Lynne knew how to entice and Mikaela thought that on the other hand that she had the charm of a potato, maybe fries at least. She couldn't resist fries anyway…

***

He was bored. Well, slightly bored. There were numerous attractive women and women who weren't so attractive, but they had assets that would make any superficial man happy. Women were so easy to read. He looked at each one as if he were studying flora. Every woman had the same likes and dislikes, they wanted to be assured of many things, their insecurities warped from time to time, and they had a compulsion for material things.

He could think of so many negatives and few positives while he sipped red wine, trying to pay attention to the lovely woman wearing a revealing little black dress, who, unfortunately was the wife of one of the bank's managers. She saw him and gave him that look and he sent one of disinterest. He had no intention of ruining his reputation as an upstanding businessman. Models and celebrities or women who weren't of this circle were an exemption. Those he could enjoy freely, without guilt or thought of business concerns.

He didn't want to attend this little cocktail party that consisted of three hundred people, preferring to be in his house to catch up on a series he had been enjoying as of late. His good friend, Michael, had other plans. Michael Smith was one of his master's degree buddies, who also had a good eye for women. The man was almost never alone, just like he was. In fact, it was Michael who introduced Jessica to him. It was a slight miscalculation on his friend's part, but that was how the dating worked. No one would fit the mold perfectly.

He wasn't here on the prowl, though. He was here to meet up with other collegiate buddies who happened to be in Malibu. It was just an excellent opportunity to meet up with Malibu society as well. The bank was an international one, and it started in Malibu. The event was small, but it was well-meaning; a reunion of sorts for very important clients and upcoming big accounts. He had a few million stashed in a two key accounts, for which the bank was grateful for. Justin still preferred the Swiss Bank, though.

He didn't quite like the canapes they served, so he enjoyed the mediocre wine instead. He was a man of fine taste, and his sisters teased him for being such a stuck-up businessman, from food to wine to women, it was complaint or disfavor. "You'll never find a wife," they would tease him.

He wasn't after a wife. He was after pleasure. California was full of it. He would move away from Malibu soon, maybe to Los Angeles, to be closer to one office. Then he would move again in a few months' time, this time in New York. He never stayed put for long and he had gotten used to the luxurious nomadic life that he had put himself in.

Justin suddenly wanted to leave the party. It was rather boring, and it was too early to have a nightcap in the hotel bar. He found himself casually leaning against a wall, quietly looking around while still pretending that he was listening to this pretty but dull woman's stories about her travels and her favorite Michelin-rated restaurants across Europe. He had tried them all, he had wanted to say, but he kept quiet, seeing someone else across him, standing alone, diddling on her phone, and obviously pretending that she didn't quite care that she was alone.

He excused himself, saying he had to see a good friend, leaving the woman's mouth agape, and she couldn't refuse. Who could say anything to stop Justin Henderson? No one. So he walked through the crowd, the women eyeing him once more and he smiled at some of them, just for kicks.

Justin had one goal in mind at that was to get to the woman who wore a cobalt blue dress. From afar, she looked pleasant to the eyes. The color of her dress accentuated her dark skin and her curls, and her heels complimented her legs, making her seem taller than she was supposed to be. He estimated her to be around five-foot-three and thought she was barely twenty-five years old. He liked making assumptions and delighted in them when he found these correct.

He approached her calmly, like he did to any woman. "Hello," he began simply, watching her scroll on her Facebook feed.

She was startled by him, her eyes widening as she looked up from her phone. She almost jumped. He smiled at her.

"Uh, hi?" she looked around, unsure if he was talking to her. "Are you talkin' to me?"

He almost scoffed at her. "I didn't know you were a fan of Robert de Niro."

Her expression looked blank. He had wanted her to smile, but apparently she wasn't that well educated with pop culture. Well, that was a sad thought.

"Just a line from one of my favorite movies," he told her, "and yes, I'm talking to you."

"W-well, I don't work here," she said.

"I can tell."

"How?"

"Because you looked uncomfortable while I was looking at you."

"Oh damn, please don't tell me you like stalking people you don't know."

"You flatter yourself too much," he said with a smile.

"Are you from here? Your accent's kind of off."

His eyes narrowed. "Off?"

"Not quite American."

"Where do you think I'm from?"

"London or something."

"I have lived a few miles out of London," he replied.

"So that explains the posh accent. Damn, I sound so posh saying the word posh." She laughed nervously and he half-liked it, and half-disliked it.

"I noticed you haven't been drinking."

"I'm bad at drinking."

"How so?"

"Like two glasses of wine and I'm kaput." She laughed with a brilliant smile.

He found himself smiling at her candidness and he enjoyed her smile. It was a dazzling smile, something he had probably dreamt of before. It seemed like she was a genuine person, like most were when you met them, especially when they knew who he was. He observed that she didn't know him.

"What's your name?" he asked.

"Mikaela. Mikaela Johnson," she replied. "You?"

He surmised she was partially educated in college. She had a typical accent, one that was quite American and her speech pattern suggested her educational background as well.

"Justin. Justin Henderson. Pleasure to meet you," he said, extending his hand.

She looked at it, quite confused. Then she slowly held out her hand and he took it and gave a gentle kiss, one that almost touched her skin but it didn't. It sent shivers down her spine for reasons unknown.

"Are you with the bank?" she asked quickly, as he stood straight.

"No," he replied, "I was just lucky to be invited."

"So am I," she said with a laugh.

"How so?" he asked her.

"Well, you see that girl wearing gold?"

She looks like a walking sequin party, he thought. "Yes."

"Well, she works in the bank, the Malibu branch. She's an account agent and one of my closest friends."

"And she would be?"

"Oh, her name? It's Lynne, Lynne Young," she replied. Then she realized that this certain Justin Henderson could be interested in Lynne, and he had probably seen them together earlier and wanted to be introduced through her. She suddenly felt bad about it. So it was for Lynne all along? She was foolish to even think he would be remotely interested in her. He was too good-looking for her, wasn't he?

"Ah." It was all he said about Lynne Young. He didn't find her remotely interesting. She was too pale and had too much makeup on and she looked just a tad bit tacky. He had thought the dress would have looked better on Mikaela instead of her. But the blue dress was great on this Mikaela Johnson. "So what do you do?" he asked her.

"Uhm," she looked shy at first. "Well, I've been a barista for a couple of years now."

"Barista?" he paused. Was she the barista with the sincere grin from three days ago? She was, wasn't she? Who could forget that smile? He certainly didn't. He didn't tell her this though, content on letting the conversation run naturally without the possible "oh my god, really?" interruptions that came out of women's mouths.

She paused momentarily, wondering if he had begun to size her whole character just by her job. She didn't belong here, she knew that, but maybe, just maybe, she looked the part?

"Yeah, barista," she continued, "At Uncommon Grounds."

He smiled. "Never heard of it."

That's probably 'cause you have coffee in hotels, or you travel to some random coffee country for it, she thought wryly. "Well, you should. We've got good coffee."

"Not the best coffee, though?"

"I think it is."

"How would you know? You've never been outside of California, I guess?" he teased.

She found him annoying all of a sudden, his good looks overtaken by his obnoxious personality. "I've been to Washington, thank you very much," she said acidly.

He gave an easy smirk. "I was joking, you know."

"We just met, how the shit am I supposed to know you're joking?"

"Do you always curse?"

"I have a dirty mouth," she replied, her lips pursing.

Dirty mouth. He almost laughed aloud, wanting to say some crude joke about her dirty mouth. This wasn't the place for it, he reminded himself. "Really?"

"Not like that!" she immediately said, reddening. "Whatever disgusting things you're thinkin' 'bout."

"So, tell me about yourself."

"Are you from HR? Is this a job interview of sorts?" she asked suspiciously.

"No, I'm just curious about you."

"Why would you be? There are tons of other people here."

"They don't interest me at the moment. You interest me. You're alone and pretending you're all right about it."

"And you're a shrink now?"

He smiled. "I can sometimes act like one. That's what years of work does to you."

"I'm no shrink and I've been working for years."

"It must be a job that isn't for you," he told her.

She paused. A job that wasn't for her? She suited in fine, customers liked her, her fellow coworkers liked her, and she made great coffee-based drinks. What else could she do, aside from hold on to that dream of studying nursing? Then maybe, just maybe, she could finally get that degree she'd always wanted.

She shrugged. "I like my job a lot."

"Can you imagine serving coffee for the rest of your life?"

She could and she nodded. "I guess I could. It has a very nice aroma."

"That doesn't sound much like growth. Why don't you make your own café instead?"

"Maybe that's why I'm here, so I can fish for a loan or something," she joked.

He didn't laugh. That was the first thing she noticed about him. He would smile, he would chuckle, but he never laughed outright. Maybe he was the serious, businessman type. Lynne wasn't this serious nor were her coworkers.

"Oh my god, are you a loan shark?" she asked, her eyes widening.

His brows rose. "Do I look the part?"

"Well, we can't ever tell."

"Unfortunately, I'm not. I'm just your average entrepreneur that works a lot. Like a lot."

She found him charming again. She thought that was the thing about this businessmen, they had some ace up their sleeve. Just when you'd think they were assholes, they'd turn out to do some charity work or shit like that.

"Justin, hi," a woman interrupted them, stepping in front of Mikaela.

Mikaela found herself rolling her eyes. Damned people had no manners nowadays. Couldn't she see they were having an "interesting conversation"?

"Hi," Justin began, wondering who the woman was. He hoped he hadn't slept with her or taken her out to a date or something in one of those rare, spontaneous drunken nights. She didn't look familiar.

"We were introduced last week at Malibu Sunset," she tried to remind him, referring to a recently opened high end bar.

"Oh, I'm sorry. Yes, how are you?" he asked, still not knowing who the woman was.

"I'm all right—" she began.

"That's great, but I'm still talking to my date here," he said smoothly. "I hope you don't mind."

The woman gave Mikaela dagger looks, while Mikaela stood expressionless. She didn't quite get what was going on. She had wanted to leave, but the moment Justin Henderson said he was talking to his date, she stopped. That date would be her. Duh.

"Why, I—" and the woman said nothing more, as Justin held out his arm for Mikaela to take.

She stared at it for a full three seconds, realization dawning that he wanted to get far away from the intrusive woman as soon as possible. She took his arm, still unsure of where this was going, but fully sure that she wanted to stay away from that trespasser. There was this sudden urge of selfishness, and she wanted to keep him for herself.

"Who was that?" Mikaela whispered, as soon as they were out of earshot.

"Some woman whose name I forgot. One of my friends introduced us and I disliked her immediately," he told her.

Wow. He wasn't one to mince words, was he? She began to feel flattered that he was comfortable with her. There must be a reason why he stuck to her all this time, when he could have just about any other female in the room, dressed much better, and looking much better too.

"Are you sure you're fine walking around with me?" she found herself asking.

"If I wasn't, would I have asked for your hand over my arm?" he responded.

She forced herself to hide her smile. She hadn't been this flattered before. It was actually a nice feeling, done by a nice-looking guy. Nice-looking guy was an understatement—he was gorgeous, but she wouldn't say this aloud or show him how she found him attractive in the least. Although, she could tell he had quite an ego.

They headed out to the balcony where they had a good view of the beach. The noise had significantly faded from where they stood. It was dark and she could only see a few feet into the beach. They heard waves crash on the shore.

It was a cold night, and she did her best not to shiver. She hadn't worn a bra because she had thought the dress's material would be thick enough. She hoped her chest peepers wouldn't show. She began to get conscious about it when he took off his coat and placed it on her shoulders.

"Thanks," she said, looking up, surprised.

"You're welcome."

"You live anywhere near here?"

"I'm actually based in L.A.," he replied. "I just travel here for work every few weeks."

"I like it here better than L.A.," Mikaela said.

"I like it better here too. And the beaches have a lovely sunset."

"What about England?" she asked.

"What about it?"

"The beaches there?" she prodded.

"Oh. It's cold. Good for cryogenics this time of year."

She looked a bit blank. Cryogenics. Where did she hear that... Ah, she had read it in one of those medical textbooks a few months back. He saw her face dawning with realization and he was glad he didn't have to explain that. His pet peeve were stupid people and he hoped she wasn't entirely hopeless.

There was a moment of silence, and he seemed comfortable in it. She didn't say anything; he might have been thinking of something important. Then he cleared his throat.

"So, I think this is an excellent time to ask for your number."

Was the how he asked women for their numbers? Really? Just like that? "What for? I'm not connected to the bank."

"Oh, I'm not after anything business related." *So she was playing hard to get?* He almost smirked.

"You want coffee?" she grinned.

"If it's made by you, I would prefer that. Has anyone told you that you have a lovely smile?"

She found her cheeks warming up and she was glad that the veranda was lit with bonfires, casting strange shadows on their faces, instead of light showing off her blushing.

"I've heard people tell me that. Must be 'cause my skin is dark so my teeth glow," she laughed.

"Don't put yourself down. You do have a lovely smile. It reminds me of Julia Roberts in a way."

She wanted to squirm in delight. She had been complimented about her smile before, but this was something different. He was different. Psshh, what was so different about him? He could have been any other customer on any ordinary day. But here was a guy, a handsome one, in a suit with a sexy accent, and the attention was solely on her. Of course she felt glee.

This was one night where she suddenly felt really beautiful. The heels must've done their work. The dress had done its trick. Those awkward hours of practicing makeup morphed her into someone worthy to be in the event.

"So, is that a yes for your number?" he nudged on.

She smiled at him coyly, wondering if this was really something serious. "You can have any girl's number inside that party, yet you're out here, talking to a barista."

"I happen to find this barista fascinating." His eyes were dark, like some smoldering secret was waiting to be let out.

He held out his phone for her to take. "You can put a fake one or you can put your real number in."

She took the phone from his hand, their fingers touching and she felt a frisson of excitement steal through her. She was going way too ahead of herself. She didn't want to look giddy. No guy wanted to date an easily-excited woman.

She slowly pressed the keyboard, punching her number in. She gave away her real number and hoped he wasn't joking about this. She would feel like a complete idiot if he was just doing this for a joke. His jokes weren't too obvious, she recalled earlier. He wasn't so good at jokes.

She gave him his phone back. Only numbers were there, she didn't put her name. Did he even remember it? "So what do your family and friends call you?" he asked. "Mika? Kaela? Mik? Sounds like a guy, Mik. I hope it's not Mik."

"People actually call me by my full name. Just Mikaela."

"It does have a better ring to it."

So he remembered her name. *That was a good sign, wasn't it?* She felt herself smile, but she didn't smile too widely, for fear she would look too eager again.

"So, I wondered," Justin began.

"Mikaela! Mikaela Johnson!" someone called out.

They both looked sideways to see Lynne Young, standing beside a pillar, the sounds coming from the party had begun to get louder. Her hair was still perfectly coiffed and her lipstick had faded a little under the lights, but she was sober and in high spirits.

"There you are! I was looking everywhere for you," she said, walking for their direction. "And here I thought you snagged a guy—Mr. Henderson?" she gasped. "Sir, good evening. How are you doing? I didn't think you'd be here. Mr. Smith mentioned you earlier."

"Well, here I am," he said to her.

Mikaela saw Lynne's smile as she walked closer.

"It's best we get going," Lynne told Mikaela, grabbing her hand and eyeing the enigmatic Mr. Justin Henderson. She had heard many stories about him as one of their most valued clients, from his playboy ways to his ruthlessness in business deals. She had seen him from afar twice, but up close, he was a powerful man, with keen eyes and a jawline that could cut through butter…

"I guess we have to go," Mikaela said, trying to sound cheery. She didn't want the night to end too soon.

"Do you women need a ride?"

"We're good, thank you Mr. Henderson."

"Have a pleasant night," he told them.

He didn't call them girls. It was women. He didn't refer to females as girls. It was always women. He saw them as equals, didn't he? She saw the look on his face. It didn't express disappointment over her leaving. It was calm and collected. Mikaela didn't look back. She didn't want him to see her face. She felt like it was her first date in high school and she was in high spirits but she didn't want it to show.

She checked her phone. It was past ten in the evening and her shift started at six in the morning. Good thing Lynne wasn't drunk or she didn't snag a guy to take her home. She'd have been stranded, then she could have asked Justin for a ride… She shook her head and sighed, hoping Lynne didn't hear.

As she and Lynne drove home, Mikaela received a text from Justin.

"Is it him?" Lynne asked, stopping for a red light.

"Mmhmm."

"I knew it. He liked you," Lynne said excitedly. "Did he ask you out already?"

"For dinner, tomorrow."

"Say yes."

"I just met the guy," Mikaela scoffed.

"You don't know who he is?" Lynne gasped. "I can't believe you don't."

"Uh, earth to Lynne, I don't work in a bank. And if he's no athlete or actor or something, I wouldn't know him."

"Well, Justin Henderson is a steel honcho. He's worth billions, not kidding," Lynne told her. "His company makes and supplies like sixty percent of all the steel in the world. His account is a bit disappointing with us, we've been trying to bump it up to at least thirty million dollars from a measly twenty."

Measley? Jesus, how much was he really worth, anyway? She had assumed he was just another of those businessmen with their usual quirks and personalities, but suddenly, he had even more reason to have that ego. Billions of dough wasn't built on niceties, it was built on ego.

"So why are you still thinking twice about saying yes?" Lynne continued, "It's just dinner, my dear Mikaela."

"I don't know the guy."

"Some of us do."

"Not personally. He seems like an asshole."

"Sweetie, people like that are always assholes. It's just a matter of handling the assholes the way they should be handled. Why do you think I'm in this industry?" Lynne grinned as she drove down the street. "I say, give him a chance."

"Too late. I said no," Mikael told her.

"Oh you shouldn't have. That's a way to nursing school. He could get you connections, a scholarship!"

Mikaela sighed. A scholarship would be great. She wasn't a genius or anything, but she graduated seventh in her high school class with sheer determination and wit.

"Oh my god," Lynne said, "you're totally playing hard to get."

"I am not."

"Yes you are. You haven't had a date in years. Why are you doing this to yourself? He's like the best potential date ever. He gave you the time of the day; two weeks ago he was dating some other model, and now he chooses you."

Mikaela shook her head. "I'm giving it time. It could fizzle out in a heartbeat."

"Not too much time. You shouldn't really do this to yourself. I think you deserve a bright ray of sunshine in your life—"

"He doesn't even laugh."

"It's your first night together. Of course he wouldn't find your humor likeable."

"I think my humor's pretty okay. It's his that ain't."

Lynne rolled her eyes as she stopped in front of Mikaela's apartment building. "Look, Milly," she said, using a nickname only few knew about. "Just date him. What harm could it do? And if he does something stupid, slap him with a lawsuit, then we'll both live the rest of our lives bathing in milk and rose water or something."

They both laughed aloud.

Chapter3

She didn't send her "no" immediately. In fact, she didn't send it at all. She had waited for a full hour and had thought he was probably asleep when she sent her message that she agreed to go to dinner with him.

He replied after five minutes. Did he wait? She wouldn't know. But here she was, trying to look her best with the most decent after-work outfit she could find, jeans and a plain white shirt. No one could go wrong with that, right? Except she began to wonder if she looked too plain. She didn't look haggard, which was a good thing. And Lynne told her to look her best half-naked.

She had asked what it meant. It meant to bring spare lingerie, just in case.

"I'm not down for that on the first date!"

"You haven't been laid in so long," Lynne insisted over the phone as they had their lunch break in opposite ends of the city.

In the end, she did, but she didn't tell Lynne. Yeah, it was for good measure. Besides, she sort of knew when a guy was attracted to her. Justin insisted on picking her up. She didn't want him to at first. If he saw where she lived, he'd totally get turned off. Well, if he really was the billionaire that Lynne had said he was, he wouldn't be too happy to see where she lived. She had gotten off of work at past three and he had said he'd pick her up by six.

He was prompt. He called her, just to make sure he was on the right street. She waved from her window, four floors up, and he saw him wave back. There was no smile. She began to wonder if her decision was all right. They could have met at the restaurant, but he was being all gentlemanly, or maybe he was being a huge showoff. His car was a sleek silver Mercedes Benz, and people ogled at him as he waited by the curb.

Dinner was in some fancy Italian restaurant where she felt severely undressed. She saw how the women wore dresses at least and here she was in ripped jeans.

"Would you care for some wine?" Justin asked her, seeing how selfconscious she was becoming. Her eyes kept darting around, unsure of herself in a place like that. "Are you all right?" he asked.

"Yeah, I'm-I'm just not used to this."

"Mikaela, this isn't even a five-star restaurant or anything. It's just a bit classier than your usual bistro. You don't stand out, so don't worry about it."

She grinned at him, embarrassed. "Yeah, I guess."

"So, wine?"

"I don't drink. Like I said yesterday."

"Too bad, they serve excellent vintage wine here."

She bit her lower lip, worried that she might upset Justin. "Maybe after we've eaten."

He was observing her observing everyone else, observing even the servers. It was a far cry from her café and he wondered if she had ever eaten in an Italian restaurant that wasn't the Olive Garden.

"You liking your food?" he asked her.

She nodded. The risotto was pretty good, seeing this risotto didn't come from a microwaveable pack. She made good on her word to drink wine after the main course had been served, so she did. The wine was sweet and sour at the same time. There was a term for this. Tart. It was tart, right?

He had ordered one whole bottle of wine and she had drunk two glasses by the time tiramisu was being served. She was finding it difficult to focus and she felt pretty warm.

"Are you okay?" he asked her, amused that someone would get that drunk with two glasses that weren't even filled halfway.

"A little tired," she replied. "Well tired-sleepy, but not too tired to do other stuff."

"What other stuff?" he asked as the waiter cleared their plates away.

"I dunno. Walk around guess. I haven't had a good walk on the beach in months."

He shook his head and gave a faint smile. "In your condition, that doesn't sound like a good idea."

They stood up, heading for the door. She did her best to control her gait. She felt her knees were a bit weak, well actually, her legs felt like jelly. She couldn't have been that drunk.

"You're walking funny," he remarked as they headed for the car.

"Just this wine thingy. That's what I told you."

"Would you like some tea to sober you up?"

"Can we just sit somewhere?"

"We're near my place, if you don't mind," Justin suggested. "Perhaps you can take a rest there before I bring you back to your place."

It was one of Justin's three units in Malibu, all were at least thirty minutes away from her apartment.

She nodded, fighting to stay awake. Did people feel extra frisky when they were drunk? She didn't say anything, afraid it would sound trivial or too forward. They headed for a ten-story building, and his unit was one of those two units that had a private elevator that led all the way to the penthouse. She was half asleep by the time they got to his two thousand square foot pad, replete with a baby grand piano, a one hundred eighty-degree view of the beach and sensor activated lights.

She stood at the door, amazed, feeling like her saliva was going to drop on the shiny marble floors. It looked like it came straight from the magazines. Her drunkenness had momentarily vanished.

"You live here?" she said, stepping in.

"Partially," he replied. "Let me get you some water. Take a seat anywhere you like."

The moment he returned with a glass of tepid water, he found her half asleep on the couch. "Mikaela, drink some water. I guess the wine was a bad idea, huh?"

"A little," she slurred. "God this is embarrassing for our first date together."

"It's a little cute and a little annoying," he said.

"Do you always do that to every girl you date?" she suddenly asked with a tone that said she was aggravated.

"Do what?"

"Act like a douche."

He smiled and shook his head. "It depends on what kind of girl I'm dating."

"So I'm special because you're being brutally frank with me?"

"Because I said it was cute and annoying at the same time?" he began. "I do that to every woman I date. What's the point of lying? It makes for a bad start."

"You are such an asshole, you know that?" she said, standing up to take the glass of water from his hand.

"Well, you're being pretty honest yourself," he retorted, still sounding calm. Drunk women were as volatile as drunk men.

She drank the whole glass and out it down on a table, missing the coaster by a few inches. He looked at the round glass markings on the table with disdain and hoped the water wouldn't leave a stain. She saw the look on his face.

"There you go again," she said. "You give off that look that you think you're better than everyone else."

His eyes narrowed. Drunk people spoke the truth and that was her impression of him when they had only met a day before. Well, wasn't she someone unique for starters? With her penchant for cursing and her easy laughter, he found himself drawn to her, amused, like a child that had seen something shiny and colorful for the first time.

He saw the thin strap on her shoulder slip down and he found himself aroused by this. He walked quickly, facing her and he held her arms tightly.

"What do you think you're doing—?"

He cut her off, grabbed her head softly and started kissing her. She resisted at first and then she moved her lips against his. One hand trailed down to her neck as Justin pressed himself against Mikaela. Their kisses grew ardent and hard. She gasped when his free hand found its way to one breast and he fondled it as they continued kissing.

She forced herself to focus. This was just her being drunk. She wasn't too drunk, but she was kissing him back. Was he drunk, too?

His hand began to skim over her bare shoulder, and she realized she wanted this. He trailed kisses on her neck as she moaned in desire.

Mikaela realized she had never felt this much lust for anyone as Justin's hands roamed all over her back, then waist, and her neck again.

She surrendered to the feeling and allowed this pleasure to steal through her. It was delicious, this feeling of being with him. She saw his eyes, burning with passion. This was the same look she had seen yesterday, that smolder, that primal lust. She didn't know he wanted it this bad, too. He slowly shoved her onto the couch, dragging her blouse down to her abdomen. Then he licked one distended nipple and she let out a soft groan as the cool sea breeze fluttered in the room.

Then he slid down, all the way down, and his tongue trailed on her lean stomach and she writhed a little. He moved his hands nearer and in between her thighs as he slid up and kissed her again. His fingers found their way into the folds of her clit and he stroked it slowly with his thumb first. She shuddered.

He slipped in two fingers and found her wet. She let out another moan. It was a moan he wanted to hear again and again.

"Oh god…" She let out a sigh as she closed her eyes. He went further down and she was glad she had changed into sexier lingerie while on a toilet break at the restaurant earlier…

His tongue teased her and she felt something in her release. This primal urge to just make love to him. It all just felt so right. He was sucking her and she moaned and moaned softly, trying to find something to hold on to and she ended up holding onto his head, actually, his hair, as he licked Mikaela over and over again ruthlessly. She had never known that a man's tongue could do this. It was an astounding feeling and waves of pleasure kept banging onto her body.

He wanted to be on top of her, he made sure of that as he positioned himself. He slipped himself inside of her and she jerked a little, loving the sensation of his cock filling her. He licked her taut nipples at the same time, and then she felt his teeth rake over one nipple and Mikaela trembled even more. Her heartbeat was so loud, she thought he could hear it. Blood roared in her ears before she had lost all coherent thought, sticking to moans and murmurs like he did.

His eyes told her all that he wanted to do to, all that carnal desire. She wanted to succumb to it.

Blood rushed to his member, and she was swollen. Their bodies rubbed against each other, their pace had moved faster. She raised her hips against him, meeting him halfway with a thrust. Mikaela panted, enjoying the tip of his member caressing her clit. Justin held onto her right thigh and continued to gyrate against her.

The sea breeze didn't matter at all as they slammed against each other, sweat forming on their bodies. He thrust himself into her harder and she bit her lower lip to keep herself from screaming.

"You can be as loud as you want to be, you know," he whispered roughly into her ear.

She bit her lower lip again, determined not to cry out for his name, as he pounded into her again and again, and again.

***

She loved the feel of cotton against her skin that was for sure. She didn't want to wake up from that lovely dream. A dream where they had made love, passionate love and he held onto her tightly, never wanting to let go. She still felt a little sore, but it was a good kind of sore, the kind of sore she hadn't felt in a long, long time.

Mikaela woke up anyway. She awoke into reality with a smile though. It wasn't a dream. She was really here, in his house, and on his bed, fully naked. Feeling a bit modest, she dragged the bed sheets of Egyptian cotton (500 thread count) closer to her body. The other half of the bed was empty, as equally messy as her side.

She wondered where he was and all of a sudden, she thought that Justin was in the kitchen, making breakfast for them. How romantic was that? She smiled to herself and didn't bother to grab clothes. She looked around and saw the bathroom door open. It was a beautiful black marble bathroom with a walk-in closet twice as large as her apartment. She saw a tub at the far end and a hefty counter and sink with mirrors that lit up the moment she was in front of it. There were freshly laundered bathrobes hanging in one half-opened closet. These were not cheap bathrobes either and she slid into one and felt she was wearing some pricey dress. She decided to gargle next and took a swig of mouthwash to surprise him with a kiss while he cooked.

Then she looked at the mirror and smiled. She had this glow that she wanted to show off. Clearly, it was an enjoyable night when she had a face like that, and it was something she hadn't felt in years. She walked out of the bathroom with a skip. She hadn't been anywhere near the kitchen. It wouldn't be hard to find though. All she had to do was follow her nose. But she couldn't smell anything remotely cooking now. She had thought she did earlier.

"Justin?" she called out, wondering if someone else was here. "Justin?" she called out again, this time louder. The penthouse suite was eerily quiet. Where was he? Was he hiding? Was there another bedroom?

She found herself in the large, stainless steel kitchen with its state-of-the-art ovens. It was devoid of people, devoid of Justin. Her eyes narrowed and she looked confused. Last night he had been murmuring he wanted her, and now he was nowhere to be found.

No, he had to be here. He wouldn't leave her just like that. She wildly looked around for him, calling out for him in a louder voice.

"Justin?" she said, stepping on the shiny wooden floors that encompassed the living room. The veranda window was open and she stepped out into the sunlight and saw the city had only begun to wake up from a good night's rest.

Funny, she swore she could smell pancakes earlier. Realization dawned on her he wasn't here. Maybe he went out for some breakfast. He would leave a note, or a text, right? She walked back to the bedroom to check her phone. There were no messages. No calls. No emails. Then she saw something on the corner of the table beside the bed, propped up against a sleek, stainless steel lamp. There was an envelope in powder blue, with her name scribbled hastily. He had pretty good handwriting.

She reached for it, hopes of a romantic explanation diminishing. There was nothing inside, except $1,000. A thousand dollars for a romantic night with her. That asshole! That idiot! She began to seethe, she had been played for a fool! She wasn't a whore! How could he? Of all the shitty things to do!

She returned the envelope on the table with trembling hands. She wanted to scream and curse. He had told her no one would hear her scream and this moment was a good moment to scream. She took a breath and wildly looked around. Had he planned this all along? She angrily searched for her phone in her bag, and when she found it, a few other things fell out of it and she cursed again.

Mikaela furiously punched for his name and called. It rang, and it rang, yet he didn't pick up. He couldn't be asleep, he had left her far too early. A headache began to form and she felt a growing embarrassment to what was happening.

"Oh my god, I'm an idiot!" she muttered, her face in her palms. She thought about calling Lynne, but she stopped herself. She saw the lacy lingerie on the floor and she suddenly wanted to burn it. She looked around the room and looked at the bed and that's when she felt really dirty. She didn't want to shower here, no matter how strong her urge was. Maybe he was a creepy twat who had closed circuit cameras installed all over to record their—his, his sexcapades.

She hoped there were none. She picked up her clothes and dressed hastily. There was a small stain on her white shirt from the red wine, but she didn't care. What was important was that she didn't look like she was doing the walk of shame that morning. It was just jeans and a used shirt, which she hoped didn't smell that much. His bedroom smelled faintly of potpourri anyway, and she didn't mind smelling like dried spices and flowers in the least.

She huffed and stashed her phone in her bag and she saw her shoes at the foot of the couch. She quickly put the sandals on. Looking around one last time, it was when she realized that this wasn't really his home. There was nothing that spoke of home in this penthouse. No pictures, no warmth. It was probably just a place where he could bring women and pay them for sex. He had paid her for sex. The thought of it made her blood boil.

She saw the envelope on the night table and almost reached out for it, taking deep breaths to tell herself she shouldn't, but that $1000 would help her greatly. Then Mikaela shook her head, allowing herself to feel such intense anger for him, that if he were to walk through the door, she could throw every expensive thing in his house at him and she wouldn't feel the least bit guilty about it.

Mikaela had never felt this much anger for anyone in years and she didn't want to see him, ever again.

Chapter4

It was six in the morning and his chin was resting on his hand as he looked on at Mikaela through the closed-circuit cameras he had installed months back. He saw her get up, looking a bit confused, then she moved about in the apartment, presumably looking for him. He smiled to himself when she walked into the kitchen, her mouth open, calling out for his name. *Yes, that's right, keep looking*, he thought, as she walked around half-naked.

As the minutes ticked by, that was when she realized she was alone. He saw her lean down for the night table and he saw that she had seen the envelope. She picked it up and opened it, then she put it back down again. What? She was too good for the thousand dollars or something? It seemed like she needed it and he was doing her a favor.

Well, that was quite rude, wasn't it? She didn't even hold the envelope again. And that was when she called him, he could see her frantic movements when he didn't answer her. He had left it at that. A thought formed in his head as he looked at his phone's screen and her name blinked every second it rang. Mikaela called him three times to no avail. He would never answer her.

He saw her dress as fast as she could, and was disappointed as he had wanted to see more of her perky behind. He did really like holding it last night. Plus her breasts were just the right size, not too enormous for his taste. Everything in moderation, except for when it came to successful business dealings and some sex-related pleasure.

He couldn't bear to keep having sex with someone he didn't like in the least. It could be in the way she looked, or how educated she was, but mostly it was in the way that she looked and the way she spoke. Mikaela fit that. While she wasn't a ravishing brunette, he found her appealing in her own, unpretentious manner. It was something quite refreshing to be with, even just for a night. But he didn't want to be just for a night. He enjoyed the sex a lot. That was the plan that had begun to form in his mind earlier as he watched her move about.

She didn't even steal anything and that penthouse was filled with expensive things. Even the sheets went beyond $500, but she didn't take anything. It surprised him, actually. She had been honest about her job, and while being a barista paid satisfactorily, it wouldn't support her dreams, whatever those were. He could tell she wanted something in her life but she just couldn't get a hold of, yet. There was also this air of secrecy in her, even if she had been quite honest with him the first night they met. She was naïve, which was one thing about her. And he found her smart, yet stupid, which was perfect for the idea brewing in his mind.

Speaking of brewing, he wanted coffee, and he thought about Uncommon Grounds, but it would be in distaste if he went there to look for her, although he did want to tease her, and see the look on her face. Perhaps he was childish, after all. He did like to tease certain women, just to see how they would react to his whims and caprices.

There was still the child in him, and his mother did say he shouldn't let this part go. Being a serious adult was part of his life though, because it was called for by his position. He was no Silicon Valley billionaire, and his offices weren't that much fun either. Even his own office wasn't filled with quirks any rich man could fill easily. His father had been a man who loved to laugh, while he wasn't. He did miss his father who had been his solid rock and source of support, but he would never admit this to anyone. No one would want a CEO with weepy backstories. Everyone liked the enigma of Justin Henderson, and magazines and blogs, newspapers and mouths loved to make stories or heighten the stories surrounding him.

He wanted to toy with that fact, which was why he had come up with that idea in the first place. Everyone expected Justin Henderson to date this type of woman, a woman that fit into his mold. Someone that was educated, well-traveled, or someone whose face could grace magazines every month and no one would get tired of it. He didn't want that, actually. But he wouldn't pass on a pretty face, maybe date her a couple of times and have sex with her, if she wanted to, which was always the case. They all wanted him.

And suddenly, he wanted her, he wanted her to be his. He hadn't known there was this part of him that existed, someone that went selfish, purely for physical reasons. He couldn't date her out in the open yet. She wasn't "Justin Henderson Material." But it would make for an interesting tabloid story, wouldn't it?

He chided himself for this thought. People weren't dispensable, they weren't objects, but he couldn't help but want her all to himself. Purely for sex. She wasn't a hooker now, was she? Perhaps he would have her investigated, maybe she was moonlighting as one and he didn't know about it. She was a competent barista, and more than competent in bed. Didn't that mean something?

No one was that good in bed, he thought, as he felt himself grow hard again. The footage showed she had left fifteen minutes after she went around his house. He was glad he didn't bring her to his main apartment. If she had thought he only brought girls here, he was right. It was meant for that. His exes lived in their own apartments, and if he was momentarily single, it was the perfect place to bring women to. That way, they wouldn't feel too trashy and he wouldn't feel too concerned about how they felt. Justin did wonder how she felt, but the empathy was only in passing.

He switched off the monitor feed and stood up, still comfortable in his pajamas, in the confines of his home. It was a luxurious house, with a one hundred eighty-degree view of the Californian coastline. The room had six bedrooms, but it stayed mostly empty at least five months a year. His quiet, large house also had a professionally-equipped gym and a theater with movie-style seating, which could fit up to twelve people.

The family room had a view of the twenty-five meter infinity edge pool that seemed to cascade into the ocean. While he wasn't too fond of pool parties, he still had those once in a blue moon for society's sake, or if his adolescent sisters wanted to jettison their friends to California for a private retreat.

He didn't bring his exes here that much, he was a bit selfish about the place and wanted it all to himself. So what he did was check in to every five-star hotel possible, or bring those exes to the penthouse if they wanted some peace and quiet, away from public eyes.

After taking a shower, he walked into his closet, which was quite large for a single man's standards. His hands skimmed over the many suits in the closet and he picked one in a navy blue. He took out brown wingtip oxfords to match his suit, and he also picked a light blue silk tie. He didn't bring a briefcase at all, just a thin laptop sleeve for his MacBook Pro.

His chauffeur was waiting for him at the entrance and three uniformed maids greeted him a good morning. These maids didn't stay in the same house. They only worked from nine until five in the afternoon and clocked out via biometrics. His home's security was top-notch, but subtle, and he had spent an additional few hundred thousand for it.

He spent odd hours in the office, depending on his mood and the workload for the day. He had a cardinal rule to never bring work home, unless he had guests who needed to be given a tour of the place, coupled with a few drinks. He liked to drink, albeit only casually, and his home had a wine cellar that housed around two hundred thousand dollars' worth of rare or vintage wines and spirits. It would take another fifty years before he would run out of liquor, or maybe for a special event like his sisters getting married, give or take ten years.

They were happily dating between the ages of nineteen and twenty-one, while he just coasted along, dating for the sake of it. He was a man, he had needs, but he didn't need to be tied down. They would always come flocking to him, even if he was past sixty, they'd still come for him, if not for his looks, then for his money. He didn't want money to talk though, but if there was one thing he learned about the harshness of the world, money spoke in volumes. Even his father, rest in peace, knew that, no matter how jolly the senior Henderson had been.

The drive only took thirty minutes, and he liked the scenic route his chauffeur took every day. There was something about watching the sun along the waters, and the surfers on their boards paddling out into the crest, and the birds flying about in the air. There wasn't much of this in England, where the water remained unmanageably cold and the air had barely any tropical feel to it.

Justin looked at his phone again, wondering if he could give her a text. *What for, right?* he told himself. He had never doubted himself before, all his decisions when it came to women were easy to make, done in a snap. But today, the thought of Mikaela unhinged him. He didn't like this feeling of actually wanting her. It was distracting for his trail of thought, and distracting for work. It further strengthened his earlier idea of having her all to himself so he could appease the distraction.

She was probably angry after this morning's abandonment, but he would make up for it. It seemed like she was a nice girl, apart from being honest. He would overwhelm her with kindness tomorrow, it could be a possible weakness. Maybe he could do it in public as well, so she wouldn't have the courage to turn him down. It was like that for some women and he hoped his calculations would turn out to be correct that she would be weak with his advances.

Nice girls like that always bent under the right amount of pressure and a few gifts. He shook his head and realized he was in front of his office building. Two days from now, yes two days, he would see her.

***

"Mikaela?"

She had just begun her shift at seven in the morning and had gone to the backroom to check on a few deliveries when her co-worker Mary Anne called out for her from the backroom.

"Yeah?"

"You have a customer here to see you."

The moment Mary Anne said that, Mikaela had a gut feeling that it was going to be Justin Henderson at the counter. She didn't want to go out, but she knew she had to. If he was buying coffee, he was a customer. If he was here to apologize, she wouldn't hear of it. She didn't want to see him at all, every hair in her body was against it.

She went to the counter after fighting against the urge to tell Mary Anne she couldn't come out to face that customer, and Mary Ann better face this customer instead. She took a deep breath and there he was in front of her. Justin Henderson. The asshole extraordinaire.

"Welcome to Uncommon Grounds," she began, trying to sound as pleasant as possible. "What can I get for you today?"

"Hello Mikaela."

His voice was like honey and she wanted to kick herself for even considering that she liked hearing his voice so much. She hadn't forgotten it but she wanted to hear it again…

"Hello, sir."

"What's with the formality?" he asked her.

"You're a customer, sir," she said. "What can I get you?"

"What did I have the last time?"

"I don't remember at all," Mikaela replied. *"I'll have the caramel macchiato with low fat milk. Easy on the caramel drizzle."*

Oh she remembered that. She remembered he had said that he liked making things difficult, probably some ego trip for this rich asshole. *Well, let's make things difficult for him*, she thought.

"I'm sure you remember."

"I honestly don't. If you please, someone else is ready for their order," she told him, looking at the woman behind Justin.

Justin turned to face the middle-aged woman, red-haired and wearing a suit. "I hope you don't mind. I'll pay for your drink. What'll you have?" he asked with a hint of a smile.

The woman looked surprised, and then flattered. "Oh, what? No, you don't have to—"

"I insist," Justin told her, his dark brown eyes looking over at the woman with concern.

The bastard, Mikaela thought. She hadn't known he could be this charming. The woman told him what she wanted for a drink, and he had the audacity to ask if she wanted to eat something to pair with Uncommon Grounds' heavenly coffee. She ended up ordering a bagel with some cream cheese.

The woman profusely thanked him over and over, excitedly walking out of the café, hell bent on telling her officemates some plainly extraordinary thing that happened at seven in the morning. She could tell her coworkers that a handsome young man had given her free breakfast and a disarming smile.

"What the hell did you do that for?" she hissed.

"I was being a good customer. I made her wait so you could remember my order."

"I don't remember your order."

"With a brain like that, I'm sure you can."

"What is your problem?" she asked him, feeling her face redden.

"I don't have a problem. I just need to ask you something."

"Can't this wait? I have customers coming up in a few." She dropped her voice, seeing a co-worker move near her to grab some tissue.

"I'm a customer, of course you'll have to wait for me."

"You didn't order."

"Is there a problem, sir?" Mikaela's shift manager, the daughter of the owner, approached the counter and stood beside her.

"No, I just don't think Miss Mikaela here remembers my favorite drink."

The manager's eyes widened, thinking he was a returning customer. Then she looked at Mikaela, expecting her favorite barista to remember this tiny detail.

Mikaela took a breath. "That was one caramel macchiato with low fat milk. Easy on the caramel drizzle."

He smiled. She even remembered his exact words. "Oh, that one. That's a mouthful, but I really like that drink."

The manager smiled and excused herself, thinking all was well.

"Will that be all, sir?" she said, trying to maintain a straight face instead of scowling. She wanted to grit her teeth in front of him, wanted to tell him what a dick he was.

"No, I have to ask you something else." She didn't think he would be this childish.

Another customer walked in the café and waited behind Justin. This wasn't good at all. "I'll call your name for your order. Thanks."

"But you didn't hear me out yet," he said. He wasn't going to allow it to end like this. He would not be dismissed.

The woman behind Justin was getting impatient. "Young man, could you hurry up? Some of us have to be at work before eight."

Justin looked behind him and smiled at the woman. "Just one second, if you please." He turned to face Mikaela once more. "Now, will you go on a date with me later?"

"What?" Her face turned pink and her ears grew warm.

The customer behind Justin smiled hearing this. At least there was still some romance in the world, and the young man seemed tenacious to date the barista with the lovely smile. She wanted to see how this went, so she said nothing, deciding to wait for the drama to unfold.

"Will you go on a date with me later?" he asked her again.

"I'm at work," she gasped. "You shouldn't ask me this."

He took out something from his pocket. A silver charm bracelet lay inside a thin box.

The woman behind Justin approved, nodding at Mikaela, signaling for her to say yes with a smile. Mikaela looked away and called for Mary Anne, asking her to take over for just a few minutes.

Mikaela took off her apron and stepped outside of the counter and took Justin's smooth hand roughly, dragging him out of the store with all her might. They were at the al fresco area of the café where no one was around, much to Justin's chagrin.

"Look, I don't know what you're trying to do here—"

"I'm trying to get you to say yes to a date this afternoon or tonight."

"And do what?" she snapped. "You'll leave me alone again. Do you know what kind of asshole you are?"

He frowned. They had barely known each other, and here she was calling him rude names. "Which part spoke of asshole?"

"You left me a thousand dollars—"

"I thought you needed it," he calmly said. "It looked like you needed it from the way you made your barista life sound."

"I don't need your money. I'm not a slut," she said in a bigger voice.

A passerby looked at her condescendingly and she lowered her voice, feeling her face heat up again. "As I said, I don't need your money. I'm no charity case."

"I just thought you needed extra help," he reasoned. "Did you even take it? I have a feeling you didn't."

"No," she sputtered. "Of course I didn't take it. You think I'm starved or somethin'?"

"Why are you so angry? If you didn't take it, you needn't be angry."

"You made me seem like I was a hooker."

He wanted to tease her, ask her if she really was, when he already had some information about her. Mikaela Johnson really needed the money. She was an orphan, she had lived alone since she was fifteen, spending time in half-way houses and at one point, an orphanage.

"If you aren't then you needn't be defensive."

She scowled at him. "I don't need your money."

"I think you do. And I think you need some time off from working. How many shifts do you do?" he asked her.

She didn't look at him. "I only have one shift."

"But you extend hours to support yourself better?" he prodded.

"I do it because I'm bored," she snapped.

"Really now?" He was looking at her, all-knowingly. What else did he get to read last night about her? The private detective had been quick. He didn't need to know about her whole life, but a summary did fine. The detective did just that.

For the lonely life she led, she sure made it seem like she came from a good family background. She was upbeat, even if she had lost her parents at a young age. She had been self-supporting since, according to the files, managing to graduate with honors. *How was that even possible*? he wondered.

Her parents had been professionals, her father was a bank manager, her mother a guidance counselor. She also had a younger brother who had been eight by the time of the accident. The private investigator had been thorough, even managing to come up with an old news clipping announcing the internment of Mr. and Mrs. Johnson, along with that of their son, Aaron, at a local funeral parlor in Washington. At least they had something in common, that he and Mikaela were quite new to Malibu.

"Will you take the bracelet?" he asked her mildly, holding up the charm.

"And what? End up paying for it?" It had her name on it. The bastard put her name on it.

"You could use the thousand dollars I left you—oh wait, you didn't get it," he grinned.

Her eyes narrowed. "You really are an asshole," she told him.

"Fine," he said. "I'm leaving this here, and anyone who fancies it can take it. I understand this isn't enough to warrant a date from you."

She looked confused, as if she was forced to make a terrible decision. She wildly looked around, trying to find a way out. What the hell was he up to?

The elderly female customer passed by, eyeing them both. Apparently, the young barista was playing hard to get. "Say yes, dearie," she called out before walking away.

"She wasn't so senile, now was she?" Justin said. "She still made sense."

She didn't say anything, but she stared at Justin as he put down the bracelet and its box on the table.

He was looking at her. "You can throw it away, pawn it, but I doubt you'll find another Mikaela within at least five miles around you. Or you can also leave it here, I don't mind if you leave it here."

She shook her head. He was leaving her with no choice. Of course she would take it. It was a trinket that had her name on it; it was something she wouldn't dream of buying in years-

"No takers?" he said, ready to leave. "I didn't think you'd be this hard to please."

"You think you can waltz into where I work and just assume I'd say yes to a date? After you left me alone?"

"To fend for yourself? In that sad, big apartment stocked with food and every amenity women want to have?" he continued for her.

She flustered. "You want me to go on a date with you and yet you're acting like a complete dick."

"That was my now-dead uncle's nickname you know," he told her.

She stopped herself for a moment. Dick was some standard English nickname and it didn't sound too well that she was comparing his departed uncle to a penis. "I don't want to go through that again. I felt used. Dirty."

"It's only dirty if you do it right," he joked, remembering their romp on the couch and on the bed. He wanted to smile at the memory of it. That night certainly had to have a repeat. At least he was sure of that.

She shook her head, he was hopeless. He was one of those people who lived by their looks and wealth. Well, if you've got it, flaunt it, right? She was torn, though. She wanted the bracelet, it had her name on it, and he was good at persuading her. It was only the memory of him leaving her all alone that prevented her from saying yes to another date.

She had issues about abandonment, which was why her previous relationships didn't last too long. The only difference was this guy had money and he was the best looking one to ask her out, yet. She was becoming materialistic, shallow. She disliked the idea of it.

He saw that she didn't say anything, or she didn't want to. He nodded, taking that as a no. This was that rare moment where silence meant no. He spun around, when she heard her take a breath. She was about to say something. That act of kindness hit through her, just the way he wanted it to.

"I'll go on that date," she began, as his back was still turned.

He didn't face her yet. He knew she was going to say something else, make some terms about it, if her flustered mind was quick enough to come up with something.

"I'll go on that date, but you won't leave me like that anymore."

He turned to face her. "I don't think we're canoodling anytime soon after that. You're not the only one that's got a lot in the head."

There was a part of her that was disappointed. She had enjoyed that night immensely. She hadn't been laid in so long. She'd never had anyone like that. He was unquenchable. She took a breath, determined to keep those lustful thoughts away.

She nodded. "Fine. My shift ends at four. You can pick me up at my place. Don't bring an expensive car. And don't dress too fancy. I don't have much nice clothing."

He nodded. "That is taken into consideration. I will see you at five-thirty."

She nodded and watched him leave but before he did, he eyes her. "Are you going to take that bracelet or should I throw it away myself?"

Her hands slowly inched for the box and she took it, clutching the box tightly. He gave a small smile. "I'll see you," he said before he left.

She watched him leave. There was a Mercedes Benz waiting a few meters ahead at the curb and he got in the back seat. He had a chauffeur; of course he would have a chauffeur. Lynne wasn't joking when she said that he was rich, like filthy rich. She waited for the car to leave before going back inside.

Mary Ann was looking at her, expectant. "So you asked me to cover for you for five minutes and it became ten? That wait had better be worth it."

"I said yes to dinner."

Mary Ann nodded. "Good. It was totally worth it then."

Totally worth it. Which part? That she had landed a billionaire that was completely interested in her or at least pretending to be? Or that she suddenly wanted to be physically worth the effort? She wanted to dress nice, but not too nice, in case he thought she was trying hard. She had nothing tastefully expensive to wear. All she had were plain clothes, great for everyday wear but not for a date. She felt a bit of panic. What was she going to wear? How would she approach this date? This was a chance that she could get to know him and a chance that he could get to know her, aside from being a complete potty mouth.

She decided not to tell Lynne yet. Maybe after the date. Maybe. Depending on how it went. She hoped it would go well. This was a real date and she was frankly getting too excited for a date when the day still had eleven more hours to go.

Chapter 5

The contract was tucked away safely in his penthouse. He had

dropped it there first, before driving over to her place in the most

ordinary car he had in his garage. It was his BMW Series 7, a glossy

black sedan that would blend in fine. He had figured he could take

her to a casual dining spot, Marmalade Café. He hadn't eaten there,

but he figured it was casual enough.

She was ready by the time he was at the bottom of the steps. He

received a text from her just as he was about to ring for her doorbell.

I'll be down in a bit. He read the message.

I want to see your place, he texted her back.

She didn't reply, but instead he found her in front of him in three

minutes. She still wore jeans, which was a shame since he liked

looking at her flawless and well-proportioned legs. She had on a

plain and pale yellow tank top which suited her fine, and plain sandals with bare toenails. That screamed she was low maintenance, which was good.

"I told you I wanted to see your place."

"What for?" she said. "So you can check out to see how tiny my place is compared to your bathtub?"

"Harsh. I just want to see where you live."

"It's this building."

"I would like to see where you live," he said firmly.

She sighed and opened the door to the apartments once more. "This way."

He followed her up four flights of narrow stairs. The building was old, but it was maintained to the best of the landlord's abilities, from what he could see. The tenants were quiet, which was a good thing, too.

"How long have you been staying here?"

"Three years this May."

"How much do you pay monthly?" he asked.

She looked at him strangely. "Why are you so curious?"

"How much?" he asked again, undeterred by her stare.

"Sixteen hundred a month, including utilities."

"Not bad for a place like this. Pretty near to where you work, too."

She didn't say anything. "Are you sure you want to see where I live?"

"And make breakfast and sleep and be lazy? Sure."

She shook her head and took the key out, and it jangled with her other keys. "Oh boy, you're not gonna like this."

"Try me."

She opened her door wide with lack of enthusiasm and Justin stood there for a moment with the sunlight filtering in from the window. He eyed the small apartment. His sisters' playroom for their dolls had been bigger in England. But it was a quaint apartment, and he hadn't expected her to be that neat. She even had a small flower pot by the windowsill.

He saw a poster in a frame, a vintage poster of My Fair Lady. He wondered why she kept that poster. It didn't quite suit her…

"You like old movies?"

She nodded. "I keep what I can. I replace the posters when I'm bored. Right now it's Audrey Hepburn. I think she's really pretty."

"So do I," he said. Then he realized why the poster mirrored Mikaela. "Eliza Doolittle is like you, she curses a lot."

She bit her lower lip. "Didn't know you were that offended."

"I just don't curse," he said mildly, walking around her the small space.

She had thought it was fine for two people, but now that he was here, towering over her, she realized her place was indeed small. She felt even more conscious about her living arrangements. It seemed like he was judging her decoration choices and her color schemes.

His eyes scanned the twenty-three or was it twenty-four square meter apartment and its contents. Obviously thrifted, some repaired, some bought on sale. Her loveseat had frayed corners, but she cleaned it well enough. Her dining table had two mismatched seats which added a certain likeable peculiarity to it. Her kitchen was tiny, with stains that were difficult to remove. He saw her single bed, partially hidden by a Chinese screen divider with its pale blue cotton sheets. Her closet was across it, a two-door closet that paled in comparison to his filing cabinets at the office.

He noticed she had no pictures of her family. Perhaps she had been too traumatized by it. He had expected to see pictures, better ones than from what the investigator had given him. She didn't even display her awards or honor roll certificates.

She looked at him, wondering if he was turned off by it. She was ready for his onslaught of coldness, for his criticisms.

"It's quaint, your place," he finally said. "Shall we go for dinner?"

She nodded, feeling strange about the whole thing. Here he was, asking her out on a dinner date, but before that dinner date, he had asked her to let him see where she lived. And he said it was quaint? It sounded so British. Quaint. It felt like a cross between cute and bearable.

"Where are we having dinner?" she asked later on as they began to drive away from the street.

"Somewhere you'll think is casual."

She hoped he didn't go through that effort to search for those cheap restaurants in an effort to be casual enough. Wait, effort was good, at least that was a mark of sincerity. Wasn't it? She wondered where he was taking her. Burgers sounded like a good idea, coupled with large fries and maybe a milk shake for good measure. That wasn't good for cellulite, nor was it a good meal to look all pretty in front of him.

They drove up to Marmalade Café. She had only eaten here once before, when Lynne had gotten promoted and she had thoroughly enjoyed it. She looked at him in awe.

"You know about this place?" she asked in disbelief.

He shrugged. "It's not like it's a secret."

"But this is you. You eat in expensive places."

"I bought coffee from Uncommon Grounds," he reminded her. "That doesn't scream five-star now, does it?"

"Our coffee is five-star quality."

"Price wise, it isn't, and I liked it all the same. Wow, you middle class people judge us right away and try to make us feel bad," he remarked.

She looked offended but decided to ignore it. She did sound like she judged him.

He decided to change the topic. The more he was agreeable, the more she would agree to what he had in mind. "You're not wearing the bracelet."

She looked at her wrist. She had tried it on earlier while dressing up, but she thought she was going to look tacky and overeager to wear it on their first dinner together. Mikaela wanted to tell herself she was putting too much hope into this date, that there was still some part of her that screamed to warn her that he was a jerk. Still, there was this tiny spark of hope left for it to turn out all right.

"I didn't want to lose it," she replied.

They took a seat and she scanned the menu. Well, at least the prices hadn't skyrocketed. She could afford to eat here at least once a month, based on her budget.

"Order whatever you want," he told her. "No more wine here, though."

She smiled at him and he wondered if she would still smile the same way once he showed her his proposal. Matters like those needed to have proper documentation…

She ordered the lobster and shrimp linguine, while he had some Baja Ciopinno, an interesting mix of seafood in a rich tomato broth. They ate in silence, with the occasional question here and there, and Mikaela felt discomfort because she knew he was looking at her intently.

"You know, I'm eating."

"So am I."

"Well," she began, "it's awkward when someone looks at me while I'm eating."

"You're not used to it. How can you be not used to people looking at you? It's like you don't have family in the least that annoys you during dinner."

She stopped halfway.

"Did I say something inappropriate?" he asked, his dark eyes staring into her light brown ones.

She slowly shook her head. "It's nothing."

"I said something," he insisted.

She shook her head again.

"Tell me about it so I can apologize for whatever mean things I may have mentioned."

Him, apologize? Please. She shook her head for the third time. She looked into his eyes and took a deep breath. "Well, my family's gone."

"I'm sorry to hear that," he quickly said, with a trace of indifference.

She felt more annoyed by his indifference than by what he had said moments ago. "It's nothing," she said, playing along.

He saw that she had finished her meal. "Would you like some dessert?"

She shook her head. "I'm good."

"What do you want to do next?"

She stared at him, suddenly imagining ripping his clothes off, just so she could hear him moan her name like he did that night… She shrugged. "Go home, I guess. Got work tomorrow."

"How's about a nightcap at my place?" he suggested.

"You said no more alcohol."

"Here," he corrected.

She sighed. "Fine. Only one glass. Are you bringing me to your harem place again?"

He scoffed at her. "I happen to like that penthouse."

"Then why don't you sleep there?"

"I sleep somewhere else, depending on work," he told her smoothly.

"Right, that's where you usually take the women you sleep with to."

"Like I said, we're not sleeping together tonight." *Not until we've made arrangements.*

She didn't say anything as he drove along the coast, taking a more scenic route to his penthouse. He didn't disturb her, so she'd feel less suspicious. Besides, he liked silence too. It was a welcome respite from work.

Mikaela saw the building come closer. It was here that she had made love to him, or maybe in his thoughts had a good bang. *Well, you're not making love to someone you don't love*, she reasoned. His penthouse was the same as she had left it, except this time, there were fresh flowers in the foyer. Finally, some semblance of warmth, right?

He quickly lit the fireplace with the terrace doors wide open for a cool night breeze. She sat down on a comfortable couch, facing the city view and a faint outline of the shoreline. He brought over two glasses and a chilled bottle of wine.

"I really don't want to drink," she sighed.

"I don't want you to, actually. I'm just being hospitable. Besides, I'd like you sober for a decision."

"What decision?" her head snapped up.

He smiled and opened the bottle of wine, pouring some for himself. "I have a proposal."

"Spill it."

"I want you to read it."

Was he for real? Read what? Then he handed her a folder. She didn't like the sound of this at all. She opened the folder and read a few sentences.

Sexual Consent Form

Right of Privacy Agreement

I _____ hereby declare under penalty of perjury that I am over 18 years old. I further declare that this agreement is of my own free will and that neither I nor anyone near or dear to me has been threatened with harm or embarrassment. Both parties agree that this is a private agreement not to be disclosed to third parties except...

She looked up. "Are you shitting me?"

He shook his head. "Of course not. This is for both our safety. Which is why I needed you sober."

"This is your idea of a nightcap?" Her face heated up. And here she had thought it was going to be a romantic end to the night, even if she didn't want it to end so soon.

"Don't dismiss it right away. Read it, it isn't much. I'm not into BDSM or anything close to that."

She was furious. "You actually think I'm a damned hooker or something, huh?"

"The something part is vague. Can you specify? Joking aside, I think it's worth reading. You'll find it's beneficial."

"Like I'm your sex slave?" She was flabbergasted, but she read on, wondering what other bullshit he had put here.

{Name}, known as "First Party," agrees to enter into this contract with {Name}, known as "Second Party" on {date}.

Terms of Agreement

a. This agreement is defined as a physical arrangement to engage freely in uncommitted sex upon the needs and wants of First Party.

She raced through the two-page contract, her eyes widening with every provision there was.

Full discretion must be maintained.

Because who would want to tell the world they were in an exclusive sexual contract, right? She looked at him with wide eyes and he nodded, prodding her to continue reading.

First Party agrees to pay for Second Party expenses, including, but not limited to: lodging, shopping expenses, and travel.

"You're really going too far here," she said.

"I think it's an excellent win-win situation," he began, standing in front of her with a glass of red in one hand. "We're free of STDs, your life will be significantly easier with my financial help—"

"So you can treat me like a goddamned sex slave."

"Cursing is also in the provision and I'm against it," he told her.

She scanned the contract again. Sure enough, she missed it, even if there was no fine print.

"Besides," he added, "this is consensual. Think of what you want to do with your life. How will you achieve that as a barista now? Well? What do you really want to do?"

"Study nursing," she said in a quiet voice.

"Study, yes, it's like a scholarship. I'd like to maintain a good lifestyle for you while this contract is viable."

"And when it ends? When will it end? There's no mention of it here. When you're tired of me? Is that it? Then you'll just throw me out and shit like that?"

His eyes narrowed. "Your mouth is too beautiful to keep cussing."

She bit her lower lip, conscious of the words flowing out of her mouth now. She took a deep breath. "What happens when it's over? It's only over when you say it is or when I say it is?"

"Trust me, you wouldn't want to say it's over. Of course I'll say it's over, but it doesn't mean I won't give you enough support. Think of it as a starter kit. How does give grand sound for when I choose to end this contract?"

"Five grand?" she frowned.

"Is five thousand not enough for your primary needs?"

"That means I'll have to get another apartment and I'll lose that money as an advance drawing," she reasoned, suddenly thinking about the future end of the contract.

He was silent for a moment and he stopped pacing. "You're right. What about ten grand? I'm sure that's enough for a month, right?"

She didn't say anything. She would be a well-kept woman as soon as she signed this contract, and also she had to be there at his beck and call. She had to be there when he became horny, in short. "You really think I'm your personal slut, don't you?"

"I'd like to say we're exclusively having sex."

He looked at her questioningly and she felt the need to defend herself. "I don't have sex with just about anyone," she said with a hardened jaw, "And I don't go around searching for that kind of satisfaction."

He nodded and sighed. "Yes, you don't seem the type."

Private investigation records showed she only had two boyfriends, one in senior year and one a year ago, a car mechanic. These relationships had lasted a year each. He didn't want to let the contract last that long, seeing it wasn't an exclusive dating contract. Maybe three months at most. Just enough for him to tire of her, and for her to enjoy what he had to offer.

This was the first time he had done something like this. For reasons he couldn't summarize completely, he had made an exclusive sex contract. Friends with benefits was out of the question. They shouldn't even be friends in the first place. He had a seen a movie like this once, a European film about a man and woman who didn't know each other's names yet they met up for sex as often as they could until it all fizzled away.

Not saying that he wanted to emulate it, but it was something interesting to add in his calculated life. A bit unusual, but that was one step out of the comfort zone. *Hey, I'm a billionaire, I do what I want as long as I don't kill, rape, embezzle, or do drugs.*

"I'll add this to the contract, then," he said, "for good measure. If I ever cheat on you, I'll give you twenty grand. How does that sound?"

She was silent. She wanted to say yes, but she didn't want to. There were two sides tugging inside her head. She saw him take out his laptop and he placed this on a wooden table that had a printer on it, adding a provision.

"What else?" he asked.

"I want you to put the time there."

"What for?"

"I think it's better if there's a timeline. This is a weird project anyway; any project should have a timeline."

He nodded. "You're correct on that matter. How does three months sound?"

She shrugged.

"Will you be able to enroll for classes within three months?"

She nodded then. "It's almost September. I can."

"Good." He nodded, typing in a few words. Within minutes of changing the contract, he had another printed again, a total of two copies for each of them. She read through the contract one last time and held it tightly with both hands.

"Still having qualms?"

She looked at him. "I need another day or two to think about this."

"You're telling me this now?" he said, cocking his head sideways. He controlled his irritation. "Fine. Two days and that's it. If you don't want any part of it, just call me before ten in the evening on Thursday so we won't waste both our time."

She nodded. "I'd like to go home now."

"Of course."

Chapter6

She signed the contract the day after, but she didn't tell him yet. She mulled things over while showering, while she was at work, and she mulled things over some more while going home. She thought about the money. She would need it. It was going to be exclusive and emotions weren't going to be involved. That was impossible of course, but she thought he would be difficult to love while she gave love freely. It was a good thing that he was an asshole. That would make things easier for her.

To accept this meant she could save the remaining money she needed for a full two years of nursing school. That was what pushed her to sign the contract. He didn't even ask her to pay for anything, in the event she had sexual relations with other people. She still wouldn't do that, that was her redeeming quality, she told herself. *I don't sleep around.*

The contract meant she would be having more sex. She thought about what made her different from the many others (she assumed there were many women), when it came to that prowess. It was something she should be happy about, right? After a long drought, after quite a lengthy abstinence. He was great in bed, and it was something she couldn't deny. She felt horny at the thought of him stripping out of his clothes, so she shook her head. *Focus, Mikaela. Focus.*

Would he pay for her rent here, too? Or would he ask her to quit her job at Uncommon Grounds so she could oblige him the moment he called out for her? He wouldn't be that unreasonable, right? He was a businessman. Of course he wouldn't be that stupid. She needed to work. There was a future without him, seeing it was only going to be a maximum of three months with him.

She also said yes because he was attractive, but the contract had said they shouldn't be seen together, and if they were, it was deemed casual. No dinner dates, no dress-up dates. The contract didn't say that she could stop seeing other guys, though. The contract was purely sexual.

Maybe that was another reason why she said yes, a deviation from the ho-hum life she had been accustomed to. A lot of things could happen in three months, and she hoped liking him beyond what was manageable wouldn't happen. *It won't*, she told herself confidently as she took out her phone to call him.

"Yes?" he said harshly.

"I signed it," she told him.

There was a momentary silence on his end. "All right. I'll pick it up tomorrow before your shift starts."

"At, what, five-thirty in the morning?" she said with a frown.

"What time does your shift start? Seven?"

He guessed correctly, or maybe he was a brilliant stalker, she thought.

"Yes, seven."

"All right. I'll be there at five-thirty."

She groaned. She liked to lounge around in her underwear at that time. She only started moving, and was completely up and about by six. "Fine," she huffed.

That meant she had to be completely fresh by at least five-fifteen. That left her with seven hours of sleep.

"I'll see you," he said.

"Yeah." She sounded lame, but she ended the call and thought about what she had done. Regrets come last, don't they? But she didn't feel any regrets whatsoever. It was more of looking forward to adventures she hadn't had yet. She told herself there was a reason they had met that night, a reason why he was interested in her. Maybe she was one of those rare black girls at the event, maybe it was her smile. *Could be my smile*, she thought, *because people like my silly wide grin.* Or maybe it was the dress, or those heels. Lynne was probably right about her looking good in those heels.

She could wear more heels, if the stipulation included being seen together. Wouldn't they make a great-looking couple? She imagined it in her head and it immediately dissipated the moment her eyes landed on the contract once more. There were rules to follow, her head couldn't be up in the clouds so often. But she rarely was this imaginative for someone who was chirpy most of the time.

She thought about the stipulations in the contract; these sounded simple enough, but she knew these weren't easy to do. She had never been that adventurous. Her move to California from Washington filled her with much trepidation. This was her chance, right? Who knows which country she was going to go to?

She had never been out of the country. She had taken a few road trips with Lynne, and she enjoyed it a lot. They had promised to go on a trip abroad together but it hadn't happened yet, not with Lynne's workload and hers. That had been a two year promise in a making. With Justin in the picture, she figured she could fulfill half of that promise. Would he allow a trip abroad if she asked for it?

First Party agrees to pay for Second Party expenses, including, but not limited to: lodging, shopping expenses, and travel.

She could swing a few things into her favor. There was nothing in the contract that said she couldn't request for certain things, like trips abroad. She didn't know how rich he was, didn't see the extent of it, but she had an inkling that his billionaire reputation wasn't all made up.

Her phone rang. It was Lynne.

"Where are you?" Lynne asked.

"At home, of course."

"Great. So I just have to tell you this, remember at the party, I said hi to this old man and his wife."

"The old man whom you said had the hots for you?"

"Oh, he was just looking at me like I was the most desirable woman there. But yeah, that guy."

"Please don't tell me you slept with him," Mikaela groaned.

"God no! He's gross. I just needed that account. And it so happened, he has a nephew. A damned successful one."

"Does the damned successful guy have a name?" Mikaela said with a laugh.

"Yes. He does. Does the name Henry Nichols ring a bell?"

"Do I look like I work in a bank or something? Of course I don't know who that is."

"He's into stocks. Anyway, old guy, well, Mr. Harry, goes, I have someone I'd like to introduce you to. In my head, I think, oh great, it's going to be another man old enough to be my dad. But in comes this man in a suit, with his dark wavy hair and five o'clock shadow."

"And that would be Henry?"

"He's the most gorgeous thing I've seen in my life."

"You always say that to anyone you think is viable for you."

"Oh my, deep words again," Lynne laughed. "But yes, he's gorgeous. And rich."

"Which is more important?"

"Both of course! But if I really had to choose."

"I'd go for a rich guy," Mikaela finished for her and she heard Lynne laugh again. "So any updates with the guy?"

"We're going on our first lunch date tomorrow."

"Good for you."

"Any update with Justin Henderson?" Lynne teased.

"No," Mikaela quickly said. "Tell me how your date goes?"

"I'll call you as soon as we're done and stuff. Can't wait!" she shrieked.

Mikaela smiled as Lynne ended the call. She was happy for her friend, but knew about Lynne's track record. With her looks, she never ran out of dates. Every time Lynne was excited for some prospect boyfriend, these relationships would fizzle out as quickly as they had started. And Lynne would cry and get over it quickly with the next guy that came along.

She couldn't be like Lynne. There were some things that she could never do, like date at least four guys in a span of two months. She wanted things to last, wanted good emotions to last, which explained her previous relationships and those all lasted for a year at least. Mikaela felt bad about not telling Lynne again about the current happenings in her life. It sounded too sleazy though, poor decision making. Even Lynne wouldn't bother with a contract. But Lynne didn't need money for school.

Mikaela looked at the contract again, determined to make things work for her, no matter the contents of their agreement.

***

The deal had pulled through; it was a difficult acquisition but his corporation was now a billion dollars richer. A good pull to the existing twenty. All for steel and construction materials. His father had turned his grandfather's little hardware store in Kensington into a global conglomerate in twenty years, and he felt the constant pressure to maintain its status.

He was doing this not only for his father's legacy, but for his sisters' and his mother's as well. They were the only family he had left, aside from those annoying relatives his father had. Those relatives tried to mess with the company and he had no relatives directly involved in Henderson Steel. He was wary of help from other people, unless he knew their conditions when helping. That contract was a part of his business personality, after all. It was for good measure, with terms and conditions set, Mikaela knew what to expect from him and vice versa.

His phone rang. He hadn't expected her to cancel this soon. She wouldn't dare, right? He hesitated to answer it at first. Then he told himself she had signed the contract. Like he had assumed.

"Yes?" he said, sounding harsh without meaning to be harsh.

"I signed it," she said with a breath.

He was quiet at first, but then he smiled. "All right. I'll pick it up tomorrow before your shift starts."

"At, what, five-thirty in the morning?" her voice sounded hesitant, like she didn't want to see him so early.

"What time does your shift start? Seven?" he asked her. He wanted to catch her off guard. Well, not totally off guard, but when she was at her most vulnerable, a recently awoken person was pretty vulnerable. He knew when her shift started as well.

"Yes, seven."

"All right. I'll be there at five-thirty."

"Fine," he heard her groan.

"I'll see you," he said. He wondered what she was planning to do. She would most likely wake up at five in the morning, just so she could look presentable.

"Yeah."

A forced reply, but he didn't mind. Justin kicked off his shoes and elevated his feet up on the coffee table. The day had ended well. A business deal and a contract signed, everything was coming up roses. That was why he was CEO. He made things go his way. He didn't want to get too excited. He still had to sleep. He would get excited in the morning.

***

She had barely stepped out of the shower when her doorbell rang. She wondered who let him in so early in the morning. She knew it was him. He rang it only twice, in deference to her neighbors who were still sleeping.

She opened it, flustered, her hair still damp and all frizzy. His eyes widened a little, seeing her in her bathrobe. She noticed this and she held onto the top part, afraid she was showing too much cleavage so early in the morning.

"Hello," he began. He was dressed in a plain gray shirt, jeans, and sneakers which surprised her.

"Hi. Wow, you really are on time," she said.

"Time is money."

"I bet."

"You don't need to act like I haven't seen you naked," he remarked as he walked into her apartment.

She closed the door behind her and frowned. "Can I get you anything except coffee and food?" she asked.

He smiled but he didn't show this to her. "I just need the contract."

She walked past him and reached for a folder on her dining table. "Here," she shoved it into his hands.

"Excellent," he murmured.

Then he looked at her, his eyes in heat. She knew what that dangerous look was. She wouldn't want anything to do with it, not this early. She slowly backed away but his hand shot out for her wrist and she looked into his eyes again.

"What?"

"You look nice in that bathrobe. But I think you'd look better without it," he crooned.

His hand ran up to her neck, slowly dragging it down to her collarbone delicately and she controlled her breathing and her heartbeat. She couldn't. He didn't need to fight for self-control. The contract had been signed and he knew this was going to be consensual despite her initial hesitation.

She froze in place as his fingertips traced her collarbone and she could feel the hairs on her nape stand from this sensitive feeling. He pulled her close to him, the thin bathrobe didn't help at all. Her nipples were hard from the cold, but they were going to be hard for another reason in a few seconds.

She was about to say something to stop him, but he cut her off with an open-mouthed kiss. She responded almost immediately, even if these seemed chaste compared to when she was drunk a few days ago. He held onto her neck, his tongue gliding down her sensuous throat, and she held in a breath, closing her eyes as she felt it.

Justin planned to stroke the anger away into a different kind of heat, the kind of heat that could wake her up completely in no time. He pushed her back, guiding her all the way to her bed. Then he pressed her against the sheets, her bathrobe hiking up further to her thighs. He felt himself harden, and he made no secret of this as he pressed himself against her thin robe.

Mikaela's chest was bared now and cool air fluttered onto her breasts. He jerked her robe down, so he could get a better view. His gaze devoured every inch of her. He wanted to have a good breakfast today, and he liked what he was seeing so far.

Her heart was racing. The contract had begun. He was getting what he wanted, the first of many of those days of unadulterated pleasure. She didn't want it to be this soon, but she couldn't resist. The way he held onto her, he possessed her. He took off his shirt and she glorified at the sight of those muscles. She had thought he was skinny, but it turned out he was lean. Now she was sober enough to remember every little detail.

Justin bent his head down and held onto one breast greedily and she gasped the moment he began to lick one nipple. She would never stop him now. He licked her other breast and she gave another gasp, louder this time. He was using every ounce of his control to stop himself from entering her too soon. She needed to feel everything was good, so this could happen again and again.

She was fumbling for his jeans, wanting to free his hardness and he quickly unbuttoned his pants and with a grunt, kicked them off with a bit of difficulty. She could see his manhood strain against his boxers and as he straddled himself against her body, she reached out for it.

He moaned the moment she held onto it, stroking it slowly. She wasn't adept, but she had made him feel sensations he wanted. He stopped her, not wanting to cum too soon. He held both of her hands above her, against a pillow and proceeded to kiss her again, rougher this time.

Without warning, he slipped a finger into her and found her very wet. Her stomach fluttered and she shuddered at the pleasure his fingers elicited as he slipped in one more. He wanted her horny. He wanted her to want him so bad that he wouldn't need to ask for it again.

Her body was supple and she was beautiful in the early morning light. He hadn't realized she was this beautiful without makeup on. It was a fresh look and he liked it. His leg shifted and Mikaela felt the tip of his penis brush against her thigh. It was already slick, ready to enter her. She made a mental note to have a good Brazilian wax soon...

His tongue found its way to the underside of her breast and then he sucked on it and sucked on the other breast hard. Her chest heaved. She heard him fumble for something and found he was now wearing rubber. He shifted his legs, positioning himself in between her thighs. He felt the heat come from her pussy and he wanted to tease her, build up anticipation. Justin teased her clit with the tip of his cock, rubbing it again and again. He saw her bite her lower lip and she wriggled underneath him, growing impatient. He saw wetness glisten on her pussy's lips and knew she was ready.

He rammed himself into her, her eyes flared from the sudden pleasure. He held onto her shoulders as he pushed deep inside her, again and again. A moan tore from his mouth, and she knew he was enjoying this as much as she did. He hadn't felt this much lust for anyone. He pushed her legs apart, roughly and she said nothing, but her grip on his back said it all.

They panted, their bodies attune to each other this time. She thrust her hips to match his pace. She worked her muscles to coax him into a climax, and the friction had become too much for her to focus on helping him. He gave one last big thrust, and Mikaela did all she could to keep quiet.

He wanted to own her, if only he could. That contract for three months suddenly didn't seem enough. He wanted more of her, but he had brought along only one condom. And here he thought he wasn't going to get greedy. She didn't come, but he did. He had wanted her to come. Maybe next time. He had months to go. Slowly, he pulled out of her, holding onto the condom, his mind returning to its normal conniving state, a politer man resurfaced, as opposed to the animal that ravaged her earlier.

Her bed was in disarray and he lifted himself off the bed to dispose of the rubber. Mikaela sat on the bed, wondering how the passion died so quickly the moment he came. A wave of disappointment crashed into her all of a sudden. Then she looked at the clock, realizing she was going to be late. She bolted out of bed and changed into her plain white shirt and black jeans. She had never been late and today seemed like the first.

He noticed her panic. "I'll drop you off," he said casually.

"I'd like to keep my job," she mumbled.

"I'll drop you off a block away. This is partially my fault you'll be late, anyway."

Partially? It was his fault. She didn't want an early morning romp. She had focused on giving him the actual contract and not enacting on the contract the first day. Could she claim she couldn't help herself? The way he touched her made her actually want to be late earlier, in fact she didn't care if she did half a day if she could have sex the whole morning.

She said nothing, controlling her anger. Sex was a good way to start the morning, in fact, she had never felt more awake. Being angry was not a good start, however.

"I thought you didn't want to be seen with me," she said, as they got into his car.

"That's why I'm dropping you off a block away."

She gritted her teeth. He wasn't much of a gentleman now, was he? The rest of the car ride was in silence. When the street before the café came, he looked at her without much emotion.

"Have a good day at work," he said simply.

She felt foolish to even expect a peck on the cheek from him. That was what couples did, not two adults who had extra benefits to their strange relationship. They weren't even friends, how could it be called friends with benefits?

What? That was her goal now? To actually be friends with him to make "friends with benefits" real? She was twenty minutes late and she realized her wet hair hadn't been combed in the least bit. She quietly entered the employee's entrance, the smell of coffee immediately enveloping her. Someone walked into the locker area that was in between the pantry and the office.

"Well, someone slept in," Mary Ann remarked. "Did you stay up late for dance practice?"

"A little," she said sheepishly. She hoped she didn't have the after-sex glow she had read about once, although she wouldn't be against gorgeous hair.

"Those kids are lucky to have you teach them," Mary Ann continued. "Why don't you open a dance studio or something?"

"If I had the money, but I'd rather be a nurse."

"Ah, that never-ending dream of being a nurse, taking orders from a doctor, cleaning up crap and whatnot."

"You make it sound so dreamy." Mikaela sighed, brushing her hair as quickly as she could.

"This is probably the first time I've ever seen you late in the year I've been here."

"This is the first time I've been late since I started working here." She sighed, silently cursing at Justin. He did this. But she bent to it.

There was a part of her that wished she just pushed him away the moment he started kissing her, then she thought about the contract, and how she loved the smell of his body wash, and how she wanted him close to her in that cold morning... She shook her head to herself. Work came first, no matter what contract she had signed.

Chapter 7

The day had started of brilliantly. Justin came in his manse, fresh from a good run at the beach, sweat dripping all over his body. He was no gym fiend, but he liked to work out during the mornings, sex included. That was probably the reason why he felt so upbeat, even if he didn't smile at anyone yet. He didn't want muscles straining against his suit or shirt, but he wanted to look like he was competent enough to knock someone down. He actually could, since he had a brown belt in Jiu Jitsu. He had been practicing it with a private trainer, UFC certified, for four years now, and they met at least twice a week.

It was small wonder that he could easily grapple Mikaela into submission. The woman was actually easy to grapple mentally, emotionally, and physically. Did he have her deceased family to thank for that? He shook his head; his mind wasn't in the right frame. An ego trip was in the making again, something he tried to control. He couldn't help it. Power just came naturally to him. It was never easy to lose family, so why would he think that? He was devastated when he lost his father and he was sure Mikaela was more than devastated when she lost her whole family.

He tried to put himself in her shoes. That was why she was needy. But it didn't show too well. He could see it in her, she wanted to be loved, like any other person, and she wanted the people she loved to stay. That was easy to read. That was why he didn't want emotions included in their contract. Three months was pushing it too far, even. He had had her moved to a newer, bigger apartment early that morning, an apartment with a walk-in closet, because women liked that.

He took a shower, which eased his ego trip. Nothing like a stream of cold water to bring him back on solid ground, right? He didn't like needy women, but there was something about Mikaela that he wanted more of, aside from his lust. What was it about her? And she wasn't even his type. He liked long legged women, women who were in the same, or nearly the same circle as his.

Skin color didn't matter, he dated whomever he wanted. Mikaela wasn't even the first black girl he had bedded or dated, but she was the first woman who had the most sincere and wonderful smile he had ever seen. Was it the placement of her teeth? Or her lips? He didn't know, but he did like looking at it, and he didn't want to dampen that grin, even if he didn't laugh at her jokes or he didn't feel very pleasant.

The moment he stepped into the office he saw the conundrum and he felt right at home. Years and years of working under his father and his slave driving subordinates shaped him into what he was now. He learned well and applied it well, seeing how successful his takeover had been since his father's death. Henderson Steel didn't even go through a temporary reshuffling of the top honchos. He immediately took over with such aplomb that the business world rejoiced in his rise. He was young, good looking, cultured, and smart. It came naturally that women would flock to him and he used this (or them), to his full advantage.

He didn't abuse women, at least he thought he didn't. He treated them well, paid for everything, spoiled his dates with lavish gifts, was loyal, until he decided he was fed up with things he found wrong with them. Mikaela was not an exception to this. She was a nice person who deserved someone nice as well knowing she wouldn't survive in his cutthroat world. It was mentioned in the file that she wanted to be a nurse. Why a nurse? They worked fourteen to sixteen hour shifts to make ends meet. They faced patient after patient and doctor after doctor, all of which had different personalities. Then he thought she fit into that mold. She adjusted to anyone.

He shook his head as he opened his emails. He didn't want his morning thoughts filled with Mikaela. He had better things to think about. And that thought came moments later with a call. An international one.

"Mother," he greeted.

"Oh don't you 'mother' me, we're not some aristocratic family."

"Mum," he sighed, then he smiled. "How are you?"

"You haven't called in two weeks," Lydia sounded like a petulant child even if she was past fifty.

"That's why I'm asking how you are."

"Well, I'm fine. Aren't you going to ask about your sisters?" she asked, trying to mask a laugh.

That made him sit straight. Something was up. "Yes, how are they? I do miss the loud girls."

His mother laughed. "They're fine. Louisa and Beatrice, well, actually Beatrice is great."

"All right, spill it, Mum," he said.

"Beatrice is engaged!" his mother shrieked, it was so shrill that Justin momentarily jerked the phone away from his ear.

He blinked. His nineteen-year-old sister was engaged? "Are you sure?"

"What kind of question is that?" his mother reprimanded him. "You don't sound happy."

"I'm-I'm more of shocked," he responded. "How did this happen?"

"Well, her boyfriend proposed," his mother began with a drawl.

"Mum."

"He did."

"Who is this prick?" he asked.

"He's been dating Bea for two years, you've met the young man, Justin."

He scanned his mind. He didn't really bother remembering his sisters' dates. Yes, Beatrice was in a long-term relationship. He was a nice fellow, with a penchant for archery. He was also still in college—Oxford, if he recalled correctly.

"With the son of the Leader of the House of Commons? What was his name? Gregory Murray?"

"Yes, Gregory." His mother was delighted he remembered.

"Isn't she a little too young for marriage? She hasn't even finished school yet," Justin snapped, closing his emails by accident. He almost cursed but he controlled himself. He didn't like where this was going. Justin was overprotective of his sisters, no matter the distance.

"Oh pish posh," his mother said. "I barely graduated by the time I married your father. Besides, the wedding's not until a year from now."

"You discussed this without me?"

"It's an engagement, not a business proposal."

"Where is Bea?"

"Out. I just couldn't contain myself. She didn't want me to tell you until a week from now when everything had settled down here."

"I'd still find out."

"She hasn't posted pictures on Facebook yet."

"I wouldn't find out on Facebook. I don't have that, remember?"

"Right. Well, I'd still tell you."

"Where is this leading to?" he breathed.

"Well," his mother began, "I was wondering if you'd take a week off to see us in England? Meet Gregory's family for formality's sake?"

Justin looked at the ceiling. The answer was predictable, even his mom knew it.

***

"Where are you?" he called her at half-past six.

"Going home," she replied.

"Wasn't your shift supposed to end at five?"

"I extended a little."

"I told you, you don't need the extra cash," he said. "Wait, are you walking home? Wasn't that place ten blocks away?"

"I'm taking the bus," she replied.

"Call me when you're free."

And he ended the call. She wondered what he was up to. Didn't he have enough of sex for the day? Or did he have to go through, say, four more rounds before he was satisfied? She pocketed her phone into her coat and zipped it up. There was a bit of a chill tonight, but it made her hair behave. The bus ride took twenty minutes and she walked the remainder of the journey to her apartment.

She didn't want to call him again right away, but there was something in his voice that said it was urgent. She shook her head, wondering why she was such a doormat over him. She only did that to customers. But then again, he was a customer. Sort of. With the contract and all. Now she sounded like a major slut.

"Well, shit," she muttered as she dialed for his number.

"I forgot I was supposed to have someone pick you up," he greeted.

"No need, discreet, remember?" she reminded him acidly.

"Right."

"Why didn't you tell me earlier? Whatever it was you wanted to share?"

"I didn't want you to talk while you were on public transportation."

Was this his way of saying he wanted her safe? He was being an asshole again, but she found it bearable this time. A loveable asshole. Wait, what? He was never loveable. Not in the week she had known him. She realized she had only known him for a week and that whatever impressions she had of him could still change.

"Uh. Okay. So, what was it?"

"I'm leaving for a trip next week," he said calmly.

Leaving? How long was this going to be? Where was he going? So that meant she was free (sort of) from the contract until he came back? But she didn't quite want him to leave...

"Uh-huh."

"For London. Just a week."

Business or pleasure? With that distance, she would never know. It was only a week, but a lot could happen in a week. What was in London? Well, she knew he held dual citizenship. He had family there, maybe ex-girlfriends, too.

"Okay," she said, making it sound like she was genuinely interested. At the back of her mind, she wondered what London was like. *I would love to see London.*

"What?" he uttered.

"I didn't say anything," Mikaela said. Then she realized she had said it out aloud. Oh my god, how stupid. How deprived. She couldn't blame herself though, as she had never been out of American soil.

"You said you would love to see London, am I right?" there was amusement in Justin's voice.

"I- I've never been there," she stammered.

"You've never been anywhere," he teased. He took a breath. "Well, I think that could be arranged."

She blinked. Did she just hear right? Or was she having auditory hallucinations? No, she was assuming again. But the contract did say that he was going to pay for every expense imaginable. He might even pay for plastic surgery if she wanted to have one.

"What do you mean by that?" she whispered, knowing it all seemed unreal.

"It means that you're going to London next week," he drawled. "I'm getting you a ticket."

"We're flying on the same day? On the same plane?"

"Of course we are. You don't know your way around there yet. Then again, discretion is compulsory once we get there."

"By discretion…?"

"We can't be seen together in London. I have to meet up with family."

She began to wonder if this was true, him seeing his family and all. He didn't seem like a family man. Having a happy family meant he should be smiling all the time. He wondered if the rest of his family was as indifferent as he was when it came to sentiments.

"I-I have work," she said, landing her thoughts of a London escapade into dust.

"Well, you'd better find some excuse. Have you ever taken a leave of absence before?" he sneered.

"No," she quickly said. In the two years she had worked there, she had never taken a leave of absence, let alone a vacation leave.

"Well, I think it's high-time you take this opportunity."

"I'll do my best to think of something."

"Think," he told her. "I'll need confirmation by tomorrow morning."

"Okay."

"Did you check your mail?" he asked all of a sudden.

"No, well, I just grabbed the envelopes from the box."

"Check it. There's something there for you. Do you have it now?"

She frowned, wondering what it was. She scanned through four junk mail letters and found one envelope with an international bank's logo on the corner. She opened it and found a letter of gratitude for banking with the establishment, and a shiny, new platinum credit card.

"What is this?" she gasped.

"What does it look like?" he said, impatiently.

"You got me a credit card?"

"Your credit score is fine, but you need a card with a higher limit."

The moment their "relationship" ended was the moment she would lose all the perks she didn't want to get used to. Apparently, this came with the sex he demanded of her. She wondered how much the credit limit was and if this was another means of bullying her into submission.

"You didn't have to do this," she murmured.

"Buy something useful with it. Shop for coats, raincoats if you must. England's weather is bipolar in some aspects."

"After work tomorrow, if I can get to the mall on time."

"You will if you leave on time."

"Justin?"

"Yes?"

"Thank you."

"This is all part of the contract. Don't forget."

She would never forget, especially when everything he did was only for that frickin' piece of paper that turned her into an object. A sex object to be exact.

"Of course I won't. Thanks again," she said this as coldly as she could and she hated the sound of her voice without warmth.

She wanted to go to England, to see London, and she got her wish. It was only a matter of a week, before she would actually step on British soil. First things first, however. She had to take care of that leave of absence. This was her chance and she would take it. Her blank passport would finally have a stamp after two years of ownership.

Chapter8

She couldn't believe it. She was flying on a plane en route to London. She felt giddy, but she didn't want to show it. Justin saw it all over her face, even if she said nothing. He had booked her on first class, three chairs away from him. She drank champagne in a single gulp, even if she said she was pathetic with liquor. He hoped she wouldn't get drunk on her first international flight. He didn't want a stomach show. That would be grossly embarrassing.

Mikaela was doing this to fall asleep, knowing she wouldn't be able to have a good conversation with Justin. He had purposefully kept her apart from him, to abide with the contract. That stupid contract. What was wrong with small talk? What was wrong with getting to know him better? This was eleven hours of sitting or lying down, and having pretty, well portioned meals with flowing drinks. She was beginning to get sleepy already.

She eyed him from across the cabin, and saw he was in deep thought, his chin resting on one hand as he stared out into the sky.

Maybe this was his form of quality time, his "me" time. It was something new to look at.

He always moved about, he always had a say about things, and yet here he was, quiet and contemplating. She liked looking at his profile, his thin nose fit his CEO status well. It looked like he was a part of British royalty. He shifted and she looked away hastily, and she thought she would read a book until she fell asleep. She took out an introduction to anatomy, a small, frayed book she had gotten in a second hand shop.

She shifted in her seat, liking the feel of her new outfits. From her blouse down to her shoes, everything was new. She shopped with hesitation. She had spent roughly $2,000 on clothes alone, plus two pieces of luggage and shoes. That totaled to around $4,800, money she could never earn in a week. When Justin called her to ask if she had gotten anything, she said she spent more than she could earn. He gently reminded her he was paying for this, and she felt even more indebted toward him.

Justin was looking at her intently now, well aware she was staring at him the whole time. She had taken out a book, it seemed like a medical book and he rolled his eyes. Medicine didn't mesh well with him. Louisa wanted to be a doctor, which he couldn't understand for the life of him. It seemed he was the only one interested in their family business. This was his choice and he hoped Louisa would make a good one for her future. Beatrice wasn't thinking too well about her future, jumping into the first proposal that sauntered her way.

He wasn't flying to England to stop the engagement, on the contrary. He was there to support it, even if he didn't want to. In his thoughts, Beatrice was still that awkward teen that liked to collect tea sets and run barefoot in the grass. He wondered what his father would have thought about this and he hoped his father would think the same way as he did now.

Now that Beatrice was engaged, he felt his mother would put in subtle hints that he was at that age to marry, that age to have children. He was in no mood for that, he was never in the mood for that. He liked his freedom; he didn't want some nagging woman to leech off of his time. Money he didn't care much about, money could be earned if you worked for it. Time, however, couldn't be replaced.

An hour later, he saw she had fallen asleep. He checked his emails on his MacBook, waiting for lunch hour. Leaving his office in Malibu wasn't a big deal, the company had just closed in on a company he had been wanting to acquire. Now that he was majority shareholder, he felt confident about leaving the company to his subordinates, young and middle-aged individuals who were competent and loyal.

They had similar characteristics to Mikaela when it came to work ethics. He wished he could hire her in the company, but she had far off dreams of becoming a nurse and staying in that homegrown café. He had also made her his exclusive "date." He wouldn't call them friends with benefits. Friends were familiar with each other's attitudes. He couldn't think of any other term for it, though.

So we are friends with benefits, only I made a contract, he thought, *and she's getting more perks than she'll probably ever have in her lifetime.*

Sex with Mikaela was mind-blowing. She was lithe and heavily involved in the act of doing it. She didn't just lie there and make funny sounds to pass off as an orgasm. Nor did she roll to her side after the first round. Perhaps it came with being sexually deprived for a while. He had planned how he was going to have some, at least twice in the week that would follow. This was a long break and he wanted to utilize it well.

***

Her heart beat faster the moment Justin's car rolled up to Rosewood London. She was staring in awe from inside the car. The bleached façade of the hotel had tall, perfect columns, with beautiful warm lights, and tall windows. Everything she had seen from the inside of the car was gorgeous.

Justin eyed her carefully. He knew she was ready to bolt out of the car and flop onto her bed. The journey had been her first long haul and he knew she was exhausted, even if she had carefully applied makeup before landing commenced. When the concierge greeted her she smiled back, a bit nervous, like she was about to commit a crime.

He took it from there.

"Honey, come on," he said, with surprising warmth, holding out his arm.

She hid her disbelief. Did he just call her honey? She slowly reached out to hold his arm, as a bellboy loaded her branded luggage onto a trolley. They walked up to the front desk, with its smiling receptionists and contemporary furnishings.

Her room didn't skimp on luxury, either.

"This is my mother's favorite suite, the Cupola," he said, once the bellboy had left with a large tip in his hands.

She stared at the expanse of the room for a full minute, then slowly started walking around, her hands touching the furniture and sheets delicately. She walked into the bathroom and saw a large marble tub with a vanity mirror.

"I hope you brought a camera along. There's a lot of picturesque places within the vicinity."

She shook her head. "I didn't really think about that."

"Well, what else are you going to post on Facebook?"

"I don't really have Facebook…" her voice trailed off as she looked at the street below her. It was bustling with people who were going home, people who rushed for dinner, and people who came from shopping. "It was Lynne's."

His head cocked sideways. "Really now?"

"Yes. I don't have Instagram either."

He smiled. "Interesting. Well, you're in luck. I do have a spare camera in hand."

He handed her a digital camera with nobs and buttons that she didn't know what to do with and she stared at it for a moment. "What? It's not going to bite you."

"I can't hold that. That's like really expensive." It was more than her month's wages, she was sure of it.

"It's just a camera. Just take care of it," he told her.

She took holding, holding it carefully, like she was holding a carton of eggs.

"I'll be leaving you now. I have to get to Kensington Gardens. You have a car at your disposal. Just call for concierge."

She had a car to go everywhere she wanted? He had given her a sim card for good measure as well, so he could contact her whenever he wanted to. There was a voice inside her head that wanted to tell him she wanted to meet his family. But as what? She watched him leave, bidding her a good night.

No peck on the cheek, no hugs. Well, what did she expect? She was a contract, an entity that didn't matter unless he wanted her to matter in his life. *No emotions*, she told herself. She would only get hurt, while he would get away scot-free. She mulled over this while soaking in the bathtub with floral water and bubbles, a bath any hardworking person deserved. She would treat this the way Lynne treated her dates.

Just friends with benefits. *We're not even friends. How do I bridge that gap?* If they could at least have some semblance of a good, working relationship, then she would feel less confused about it. So it could be a legitimate friends with benefits thing.

She huffed and closed her eyes. Nothing should ruin this once-in-a-lifetime vacation, not even her thoughts, or his indifference.

***

He arrived at past nine in the evening in front of a large brick and concrete home surrounded by trees and other luxury properties. He smiled to himself seeing their home was lit up for his arrival. The air smelled heavily of fallen flowers and he realized he missed this certain scent. He didn't need to ring the doorbell. A maid answered the door for him.

"Sir," she began, "welcome back."

He motioned for his chauffeur to bring his luggage in, and he stepped into a home he hadn't been in for six months.

"Is he back?" a shrill voice called out. "Letty is my brother back?"

Letty, their loyal maid for more than ten years, looked at Justin and smiled. "Yes he is, Miss Louisa," she said in a not-so-loud voice.

He heard the shuffling of feet running down the stairs. A brunette with wide eyes and a dimple on her left cheek stopped at the foot of the stairs.

"Justin!" she cried out, enveloping her brother in a hug, all five feet two inches of her.

Justin embraced her tightly, one of the rare displays of affection he did. "Well, look at you, I think you grew half a centimeter."

"Not funny, Jus."

"Where's mum and Beatrice?"

"Mum's in the movie room, Beatrice is out on a date. Your bedroom's ready, by the way," she said, grabbing his hand. "Come."

He followed his sister's lead to the theater room.

"Louisa, did you bring in some chips—" his mother stopped midway and gasped, "Justin! You're finally here!" She stood from her theater recliner, without bothering to pause the movie, nearly suffocating her son with her hugs and kisses.

"Mum," Justin said, "you're choking me."

She let go and looked at her son, appraising him. "My, my, have you been eating well enough since you broke up with what was her name? Louisa, what was her name?"

"Collins. That model," Louisa chimed in.

"We weren't seriously dating. Where did you read this?"

"The Sun," Lydia Henderson told him.

Justin shook his head. "That's a tabloid, Mum."

"It was a fun read," Lydia laughed.

"You read gossip about your own son?"

"Like I said, it's fun."

"And it puts ideas in your head, Mum," Justin told her.

"Mum, shall I stop the movie?" Louisa asked.

"Yes, yes, dear. Justin and I have a lot of catching up to do. Care for some red?" she asked her son.

"It's been a long day," he began, but he stopped seeing his mother's look. "Fine, maybe a glass or two."

They had wine at the patio, facing the other houses that lined the quiet street. Two of their four cars were parked outside by the curb. The air was cool and his mother expertly poured him a glass.

"I hope you have time for us tomorrow. Well, the whole engagement proper isn't until Thursday."

"I have to see the office tomorrow morning. Maybe in the afternoon?"

"It's been handled fine. You know I still oversee a few things."

"You don't even like visiting the office."

"It's not the only place I get to visit when I go," Lydia said, referring to their meager thirty-five story building downtown, prime property that everyone wanted to snatch the moment other businessmen thought Henderson Steel would falter the moment Justin took over.

"Why stay in America, though?"

"Because we're fairly new there," Justin reasoned, "and I'm far away from those godforsaken paparazzi."

"You can always ignore them."

"I can't relax or date anyone properly with those cameras and nosy reporters breathing down my neck."

"Speaking of media, there will be a few media on the engagement day."

"You turned this into some celebrity affair?" Justin began, "Mum—"

"Hear me out first, Justin. First off he's the son of the Leader of the House of Commons, so that's to be expected. Second, his mother works as society columnist at the Daily UK, that's expected too."

Justin sighed. He had wished for a low key engagement party. He had nearly forgotten that his sisters were socialites, although he hated the term. It couldn't be helped, they were a prominent family, after all. For all he knew, Mrs. Murray was in on it, writing articles about him and his billionaire lifestyle. The paparazzi were lenient on his sisters though, and for that he was glad. Perhaps it was because they were low key, and didn't like partying much in public. The media liked it when one made public disturbances and embarrassments. He dated a lot of women, and according to some claims "broke a lot of hearts."

"Which hotel?" he asked immediately.

"Rosewood London."

Great, he thought. "Couldn't you have found a newer place?"

"I happen to be comfortable with Rosewood, and so do the Murrays. Beatrice was all for it, too."

Justin knew this was going to be some high tea session, with a professional photographer and knolls of flowers from Lydia's garden for ambience. He knew he would not spare any expense for this, seeing how his family was richer than the Murrays. The Murrays had to know who they were dealing with, and Justin would send this off as a subtle warning.

He nodded, knowing there was no way out of this. "All right. Any arrangements I need to make?

"All taken care of. Why would you spend a measly week with us just to plan an engagement party?"

"I thought there were certain funds needed."

His mother laughed. "Darling, you may be the CEO, but I'm the mother of the CEO."

"I'll have our lawyers draw up the necessary paperwork."

"For what?"

"The prenuptial agreements."

"That's unnecessary."

"How can it be unnecessary?"

"Bea wishes for none of it."

"What?" He was aghast.

Lydia shrugged. "She'll come to her senses soon enough. Your father and I were mad for each other, yet even we had our prenuptials."

Justin felt annoyed. This wasn't a good thing. While they were a private entity, who knows what magic these Murrays could do? Gregory was a star pupil, he recalled, so his smarts had to amount to something. Beatrice wasn't scholarly, but she was one of the kindest persons who graced the planet, atop of her loveliness. He hoped Gregory wouldn't take advantage of it. Justin would push for a prenup, after the engagement party.

Situations like that always called for a contract. Then he thought about Mikaela for a moment. Well, that one—that was a different story. He drank his remaining wine in a single gulp and breathed in the cool air, hoping for something good to come out of all of this.

Chapter 9

She woke up with a smile on her face. These bedsheets were the nicest she'd ever slept in since... Justin's penthouse. She shook her head. Today was going to be a fun day. She had no itinerary, but she thought to explore the nearby areas first. She rang for room service and while she was in her bathrobe, searching for places to explore, a butler came with a traditional British breakfast, tea included. She smiled, thanking the butler and grabbing her camera as soon as he had left. This had to go down in her history as her first all-British breakfast.

She had never tried black pudding before, that with eggs and sausages. She took a bite of the black pudding and nodded to herself while chewing. That was interesting, even if it looked unappetizing. She had planned her itinerary as soon as she had finished most of her breakfast.

Today, it was going to be at the British Museum, the Royal Opera House (what was there? She was almost sure there weren't any shows in the morning), and a walk along the river Thames. Then she would decide where to eat and maybe shop a little if she wasn't too tired.

Mikaela was quite excited. The weather app had said it would be a maximum of seventeen degrees today, with the possibility of rain. She was glad she had bought a portable umbrella and a fashionable raincoat. She wore skinny jeans, a loose light pink sweater and brown leather boots. Her trusty backpack from her college years was ready as well, with its frayed straps and distressed look, which definitely wasn't intentional.

She had just only stepped out of the hotel when she received a message from Justin.

Where are you?

About to go out, she replied.

Did you eat?

Yes.

And that was that. She lingered at the carriageway entrance for a few minutes to wait for his reply, but he didn't. She sighed and began her solo tour. She had downloaded a few maps, her camera was charged, and she had enough money and credit with her to last her for the day, maybe even a month in London if she could.

She wondered if she could still go to the Stonehenge, but according to some reviews, it wasn't worth the hours wasted in driving. Well, I have one week here, she thought. England had so much history and she wanted to soak in it. She had been a history fiend in high school, and if her parents hadn't died, she would have loved to be a historian or archaeologist.

Mikaela wished her family was with her. They would have enjoyed this. Right before they died, they had planned a trip to Hawaii. Planned. Past tense. That trip would have been a month after her brother's special awards. Well, I'm enjoying this for you guys, she thought two hours later. She hadn't enjoyed a real vacation in a while which wasn't within a hundred-mile radius, and wished she could post every picture she took but knew she couldn't. A job was important after everything had ended.

She felt hungry a little while later and found a quaint little café just feet away from the river Thames. She ate with gusto, despite being alone. She didn't act too touristy though, stopping herself when she'd be on the verge of taking too many photos. *Don't attract too much attention,* she told herself. Her personal guide wasn't here. He wouldn't be with her the whole time she was here.

The thought of it suddenly disappointed her. Even if he lived here, she wanted to share these experiences with him. Perhaps now that he was back home, he'd finally laugh. Mikaela had never seen him laugh. Sure he'd smile, crack a joke that was barely funny, but he never laughed. Mikaela thought she had a sense of humor. Apparently, Justin Henderson didn't. Did it come with being CEO? Perhaps it was a façade he wanted to maintain. Whatever it was, she wished she'd heard him laugh, even just once.

Mikaela realized she wanted to make a connection with Justin. She wanted him to like her in the least. She almost laughed to herself, almost snorted into her cup of tea. Him? Like her? The contract was made for reasons that excluded emotions, yet here she was, liking him. It was abnormal. She felt like she was back in high school again, crushing on some football varsity player she couldn't get the courage to talk to.

She realized she was veering away from her vacation thoughts. Justin wasn't a part of her vacation, he just graciously paid for it. *I'm only here for six days. I'm only here for six days,* she told herself again and again.

Tomorrow, she planned to see the changing of guards at Buckingham. She wished she could have a side-trip to Scotland, but even six days suddenly felt like it wasn't enough for London alone. It had started to rain and she realized she didn't bring along an umbrella.

She stayed under the marquee of some tea shop as she headed back for Rosewood. The temperature dropped quickly, but Mikaela felt lucky she had packed along a waterproof windbreaker. It wouldn't help much with the cold, but at least it would keep most of her clothing dry. As soon as the rain died down, she briskly walked back to the hotel.

By the time she had gotten back, her teeth were chattering from her soaked jeans. She didn't want to step inside the hotel looking like an orphaned waif, but the warmth won over her.

"Madam, are you all right?" someone from concierge asked her.

"I wore the wrong clothes," she laughed while her lips turned pale.

She realized her phone was ringing. The moment she held it, the call ended. There were four missed calls from Justin. *Oh no*, she thought. She shoved her phone into her backpack and quickly headed for her room. She stripped out of her wet clothes and wrapped herself up in a bathrobe. Just as she was about to press Justin's name for a return call, he called again.

"Where the bloody hell are you?" his irritated voice greeted her.

"I'm back at the hotel. I had to wait for the rain to stop," she stammered. She felt like a little child, caught in some petty crime. Why was she feeling like this? He was not the boss of her!

"I had wanted to have you picked up, wherever you were."

He was going to ask some of his people to pick her up? Why not do it himself? She suddenly wanted to feel important in his life.

"I was just walking around."

"And you must be bloody soaked," he said.

"A little," she told him.

"Great, because I'm right outside of your door."

"What?" she gasped.

He knocked and she peered through the eyehole to find him right outside, dressed in a suit. She gingerly opened the door. He strode in calmly.

"A little?" he smirked. "It looks like the whole of England rained on you."

"So I lied."

"I don't like it when you lie to me."

"It wasn't your concern."

"How can I demand things from you if you're unwell?" he snapped.

She was taken aback. "I'm on vacation. I was walking around. It so happens that it rains. I've got my windbreaker, I've got boots, so I'm not soaked like the whole of England rained on me."

"You sound defensive," he remarked.

"What's the point of this?" she retorted. "You allow me to go here, to have my first real vacation in years, and outside of the country too, and then you make me feel bad."

"To remind you that the contract stays active wherever you are. Now, get out of that bathrobe. I only have an hour to be here."

She stayed rooted in place, and she found herself stripping out of her warm, fuzzy, cotton bathrobe just seconds after he had demanded it.

***

She watched him as he put on his boxers first, then his pants and his unbuttoned shirt. "Where are you off to later?" he asked apathetically.

"I don't have any idea yet," she admitted, bringing the bed sheets closer to her body. Her nipples were still erect from the cold and the mind-blowing sex she had just had with him. There were so many firsts for this day alone.

It was the first time she enjoyed a British-style breakfast. Her first meal near the river Thames. It was the first time she had had sex in a five-star hotel. The first time she had sex on international soil. She eyed his rigid stomach and wondered why she dreaded the contract sometimes. He was dreamy, he was everything she didn't know she wanted until the day she met him.

What did she want from him anyway? His money? It definitely helped her. What else was there? His sparkling personality? His good looks were more than a plus. He looked good in suits. She always saw him in a suit and those expensive shoes, oxfords, brogues, and the like. Was that what made women fawn over him? Was it the sex? True, she liked, no, loved the sex. But she could live without it. She wondered if he could. Maybe he was a sex addict or something. She should have had some psychological test done for him before she signed the contract.

Well, too late for that now. What she saw was that he was a psychopath. Being a CEO, he had the makings of being one. He was calculating and intelligent, superficially charming, he read through people easily, and he enjoyed manipulating her. She didn't know about other people, but it felt like he enjoyed doing that to her. She knew about it, yet she allowed it. Was this some sort of battered person's syndrome now? Mikaela felt she had all the symptoms…

She wasn't born stupid; she wasn't born to take orders from anyone. She told herself she'd turn things around for herself the best she could. This was no exception. Justin Henderson was just another test of sorts.

"Won't you stay?" she suddenly said with a bright smile.

He stopped buttoning his shirt and looked at her face for a moment, intently. Then he finished buttoning up his shirt, without giving her another glance until she interrupted him, asking him the same thing.

"I only have an hour, and it's running up. Kinda busy today," he told her.

"You had an hour to drive all the way here for some afternoon delight?"

He smiled. "You could call it that."

She tried to hide her disappointment.

"Hope you brought a gown. If you haven't, you'd better. There's a good show at the Opera House tomorrow," he told her.

"Maybe I'll buy one," she said acidly.

"Yeah, you should. I'll see you in a few," he said, picking up the suit he hung from the chair.

See you in a few what? Hours? Days? She technically had four more days to go in London. She watched him as he fixed his shoelaces, not even bothering to make small talk with her. Yeah, because small talk was to mask the awkwardness right? Because there was no awkwardness here, right? It was just a contract being fulfilled. Yes, that stupid contract. She began to hate it immensely. Add to the fact that they both carried copies of the contract, for it was mandatory that they wouldn't forget about it.

She felt dirty again. She felt used again. No matter how much she told herself to enjoy the moment, to enjoy what he offered her, she just hated it when he did that. She hated it when he ignored her, just had plain good sex with her then tossed her away like she didn't matter at all.

He walked out without another word. He was an asshole. The biggest asshole she had ever met in her life. She seethed; she had never been this angry at anyone. She was getting her revenge, no matter how tiny it was. She dialed for the spa.

***

The opera was lovely, she almost cried. She felt glitzy and cultured, even as she watched alone. The moment she stepped back into the hotel from her service limousine, she felt stares all over her while in the lobby.

"Miss Johnson, good evening," one bellboy greeted her.

She smiled at him, that dazzling smile that many wanted to look at for quite a while. She had nearly forgotten the power of her smile. She should have used it more often on Justin. She heard a few gentlemen ask about her.

I can hear you, you know, she thought, *and I'm no model, but I feel like I'm one now.*

It was probably her dress, a number she had bought off the rack, at Harrods. It was her most expensive purchase in London yet, that along with the shoes and clutch bag she probably wouldn't use until another formal event years from now. The dress was a lovely cobalt blue number, the same color she wore the night Justin approached her, among all the women he could have approached.

She felt extra confident tonight. To fully utilize her glamorous looks, she decided to have a nightcap at the bar. If this confidence tonight could work on other men, surely it would work on Justin. Time to put the theory to a test.

As she walked into the bar, she noticed it was full of men, only two other women were there. She took a seat on a plush chair, three empty chairs surrounded her. She ordered a glass of champagne and enjoyed the tingling sensation going about in her mouth. This was good champagne, for someone who didn't drink alcoholic drinks much.

In less than five minutes, two men walked up to her, introducing themselves as Swedish businessmen, asking if they could take a seat with her. She nodded. It was working. She hadn't expected it to work so soon. She decided to revel in the moment. This had only happened when she was all dolled up. She was more than dolled up. She felt glamourous, she felt like she was on top of the world.

Was this how Justin felt when he was surrounded by a lot of women? It was good to the ego, to be acknowledged by people, to be admired for being physically beautiful. She would play the part well,

and she planned to enjoy it immensely while it lasted.

Chapter 10

Justin was irritable. She hadn't answered in over an hour. He was sure she had been brought back to the hotel. He had hired a car for that at her beck and call. She couldn't have fallen asleep an hour after the show, right? He had begun to frown but told himself not to, as he was walking into Rosewood's lobby. The lobby was devoid of guests as it was nearly ten in the evening.

"Mr. Henderson, good evening," a bellboy greeted him. Justin Henderson was a bit well-known in the hotel, he held a few meetings here once in a while and was an excellent tipper.

"Hullo," he replied distractedly. He looked around. "Has Ms. Johnson arrived yet from the opera?"

He nodded. "Yes sir. A little over forty minutes ago."

He proceeded for the elevators but he saw that the bellboy wasn't finished talking yet. "Well?"

"I believe she's waiting for you at the bar, sir," the bellboy added.

The bar? But she didn't drink… He nodded and said a curt thank you and walked for the bar. What would she be doing there? Its interiors screamed it was a gentleman's bar, but then again, she was American and didn't know about places like these. He passed by two concierge talking to themselves in hushed tones as they pushed a trolley.

"She's a real pretty one, ain't she?" one man whispered.

"Prettiest by far to walk here in weeks," the other nodded in agreement. "I'm guessing it's her smile."

Her smile. That could mean only one person. Unless another guest had that dazzling smile at Rosewood. Being in a bar meant that she was either drinking alone, or had been invited to drink. Mikaela was quite gullible to some extent, and this thought annoyed him.

He stopped at the door seeing Mikaela at the end of the room, standing by the bar, surrounded by four, no, five men, businessmen by the looks of it. His temper flared, although he did his best to control it. She was having a grand time by the looks of it, laughing at the morons' adlibs and antics. They were all vying for her attention, circling on her like vultures set on eating prey. He was here to prove he was alpha male, he was the ultimate hunter.

He strode to their direction, detesting the tinkling sound of her laughter. Were they even that funny that she should laugh at every little thing they said?

"Sweetheart," he said in a voice louder than usual.

The group looked to his direction in unison. Justin sized everyone up in an instant. They all wore department store brand suits by the looks of it, and they all had polished shoes, and distinct Scandinavian accents. Juniors at some big corporation.

Mikaela was looking at him like she had seen a ghost. For a split second there, he thought she didn't see him. Was she drunk? Drunk on attention, more likely. The men surrounding her were all smiles, obviously charmed by her. She wasn't even that charming, right?

She was at a loss for words at first. She hadn't seen him so controlled but she knew he was pissed. "Hi," she said lamely. "I thought you were busy today."

"Change of plans. Am I glad you have company," he said this with poison in his eyes and in his tone of voice. "Who are these gentlemen?" he asked, walking closer to her.

Without saying anything else, the men moved aside to let him through, with just enough space for him to squeeze in.

Mikaela forced herself to act like everything was all right. "Oh, hey. Well, this is Klaus, Erik, Aksel, Frederik, and another Klaus," she said with a nervous laugh.

"Pleasure to meet you, gentlemen," he said with a nod. One man extended his hand to shake it. He decided to introduce himself. "I'm Justin, Justin Henderson."

Their eyes widened.

"Henderson Steel?" Frederik said.

"You're Justin Henderson? Sir, it's an honor," another greeted, shaking his hand.

"Did we meet before?" Justin asked good-naturedly.

"Never had the honor, Sir. We're with Vanguard Insulation," Erik explained.

"Ah, so our companies have done a bit of business together." Justin smiled. "Well, gentlemen, order anything you want, tab is on me. We just need to get some shut-eye now, it's been a long day."

They thanked him profusely and said a polite farewell to Mr. Henderson's girlfriend, unable to believe their luck, meeting a really hot woman who turned out to be Justin Henderson's girlfriend, the number one steel manufacturer in the world. They idolized him to some extent; Justin found it obvious.

He walked arm-in-arm with Mikaela all the way to her bedroom. Once they were in, he let go of her quickly, albeit harshly.

"What the hell was that?" she snapped, flinging off her heels to a corner, her gown wafting a little as she did.

He walked up to her, towering over her once more. "That wasn't a very smart thing to do."

"I only had one drink. One drink. God, you can see it on the tab if it bothers you so much."

"Your drink didn't bother me. Your company did."

"I had a fun night, you know."

"Surrounded by those men?"

"Those gentlemen were very nice," she snapped at him, "and I was having a grand time. Far grander than being with you. You've always got a stick up your godforsaken ass."

He sucked in a breath, unable to believe she had said that. "And who are you to talk to me that way?"

"I'm under your contract, but it doesn't mean I could keep silent about your stupid manners."

"I was very pleasant as far as you can see."

"You think you own me. You think you're the king of everything," she continued. "You pulled me out of there when the contract said nothing about talking to other guys."

"They were flirting with you, you idiot," he muttered. He realized she was doing this to make him jealous. The poor girl, she probably thought it would work. It only served to annoy him greatly. She had such sad tactics.

"So what if they were? It wasn't as if I was going to sleep with them. You have the rights to sleep with me!" she cried out. "I've only met you for two weeks and you think you own me. Well, newsflash, you shit don't."

"While the contract is in effect, you're mine. Completely. And we had an agreement about cursing."

She shook her head, determined not to cry. How many times had this happened in the mere weeks she had known him? She looked at him, her vision clouding over. "You really are an asshole, aren't you?" she snapped, unable to control her words.

He said nothing and just looked at her. She spun around and unzipped her dress in front of him, surprising him. She stripped herself from her gown, and he saw she had on racy lace and satin lingerie that followed her posterior in such a lovely manner, he had to stop himself from gripping her behind.

But that wasn't all. She stripped off of her lingerie too, leisurely, and it tortured him. His animalistic urges were starting. He couldn't be celibate with her around, not with her undressed like this. Even without clothes she was gorgeous. She turned to face him and he saw she was bare down there, and he wanted to smother his face in it. Sweet mother of...

She was looking at him, as if she was bored. "I need to sleep in a bit. If you'll excuse yourself out that'd be great."

What did she just say? Did she just tell him to leave? He walked toward her, determined to overpower her. He wanted sex and he wanted it now. "I'm having you tonight," he said with a clenched jaw.

"If you want me tonight, you're going to have to listen to screams the whole time. I'll scream you're hurting me," she said with a hint of a smile. "That way everyone on this floor can hear. Justin Henderson hurts lover in hotel room."

He stopped in place. He was not expecting that at all. "You think you're so smart—"

"Get out, I'm tired. You can have me tomorrow if you aren't busy," she said coyly, proudly displaying her nakedness. The spa did wonders yesterday, she thought.

He thought about the engagement party tomorrow and shook his head. The bloody hell!

Mikaela saw his jaw hardening and she knew he was horny. *You're not the only one that can manipulate,* she thought.

Justin took a deep breath and spun around, bidding her a good night. He had been caught off guard. He had not expected her to make such a bold move. It was a move that worked. *That move gave me damned blue balls*, he thought, still infuriated as he made the journey home. He would need a glass or scotch later. He thought about how lovely she looked, and he hadn't noticed that while at the bar, and she was at her most glorious. His judgement was clouded over by the men around her. Couldn't she get that through her head that she was his and his alone?

Then he thought about the engagement party tomorrow and he hoped that she wouldn't be there. He could prod her out of the hotel, make her move out even. That wasn't too much to ask, right? She had the upper hand now. Tomorrow he would have it.

"You're drinking scotch," his mother interrupted his thoughts. "Bad day?"

"You know me all too well," was his reply.

***

It was a party fit for royalty, well, they were technically corporate royalty. The room was filled with peonies and all the expensive tea sets were out for the small crowd of twenty-five to use. The chandeliers sparkled, and everyone was dressed to impress. It looked like a 1950s movie had come to life.

The women in his life had never looked lovelier, and despite his glum outlook about his sister getting married, he was fairly happy with how George treated Beatrice. The smallest things mattered to Beatrice and it mattered to him, being the remaining father figure and older brother. Pictures were taken and gifts piled up despite the small crowd.

A sizeable paparazzi group had wanted to enter hotel premises, but no one would let them. Security was excellent and Justin realized this was why his mother and George's parents wanted the party here. Sunlight filtered from the tall, rectangular windows. It was a good day for a party and a shoot in the small garden the hotel had.

He suddenly wondered what Mikaela was doing. Where she was, if she was awake already, seeing it was nine. Of course she would be, she was used to waking up early, and she could be cramming in every possible sight to see while she had two days left in London. He only had sex with her once on this trip and it was bothering him already, plus his ego had been ticked off. Without another thought, he reached for his phone and texted her.

It took her awhile to respond.

Still in my room. I see media outside trying to get in the carriage way entrance.

Yes, they're bothersome. Where are you off to today?

Saw Big Ben, changing of guards, Westminster, and Tower of London already. Thinking about Stonehenge.

God no. You can't even get close to it. It's a waste of 6 hours of driving back and forth.

I'm not the one driving anyway.

Mikaela was eating breakfast as she replied, picking up a newspaper, and the second among three dailies that morning. She saw a photo of Justin and stopped.

"Beatrice Henderson of Henderson Steel Engaged to Murray Son," said a society news headline. Underneath the photo was a caption, *Seen here with sister Louisa, billionaire playboy brother Justin and mother Lydia.*

She almost laughed. Playboy brother? The colored photo was recent, she figured. So that's why he was here. His sister was about to get married. He didn't bother telling her about that. Wasn't that kind of happy news worthy of sharing?

Well, maybe not to me, she added as an afterthought. She didn't mean much to him anyway. *No, I'll mean something to him. I'll make it happen.*

As it was a sunny day, she opted for a pale yellow dress and black ballet flats. She now carried her raincoat and umbrella safely in her new messenger bag. She opted for a museum walk, and maybe add a bit of shopping if she wasn't too exhausted. An Egyptian show was on loan from Cairo, which made it all the more exciting. She did want to take a peek at the engagement party and it was sure to be at the Rosewood, seeing how curious the paparazzi were piqued her curiosity, too.

Mikaela made her way down, conscious that she wasn't really going to crash into a party, she just wanted to see how it was like, an upper-class British occasion with tea and expensive tea sets and the like.

There was no signage to indicate an engagement party was taking place, but Mikaela found herself walking for a small event room she had seen on her first day of exploring about. It seemed a likely place. She opened the door ever so slightly when a voice interrupted her and she almost jumped back.

"What are you doing?"

She spun around to see Justin, wearing a summer suit, with a navy gray top and khaki colored slacks and brown oxfords.

"I-I was just walking around, stretching my legs," she stammered.

His brow rose. "You're a bad liar."

"I didn't know you had an event here. I just saw the door open and there were flowers everywhere and the tea sets—"

"Didn't know you liked tea sets."

"They're really nice to look at."

"Don't you have London to see?"

She nodded when the door opened wide.

"Justin, I was looking for you—why, who is this lovely young lady?" Lydia Henderson began.

Mikaela felt like a deer caught in the headlights. She saw in front of her a middle-aged, yet slim and beautiful, brunette-haired woman wearing a pastel A-line dress with a string of pearls on her neck. She could have passed for Justin's older sister.

"She's—"

"Mikaela, Mikaela Johnson," she smoothly cut Justin off before he could dismiss her presence. "Justin and I know each other from California."

Lydia smiled, seeing how pleasant this young woman was. At least this one had manners. The others pretended to have manners but their true colors showed in the end. She had seen enough of Justin's dates to last her for a year at most. She looked like a modern Dorothy Dandridge, she had this invigorating quality about her, a down-to-earth manner and the most gorgeous smile Lydia had seen in recent memory. Were they dating though? It didn't feel like it, but Lydia suddenly wished they were.

"California?" Lydia smiled.

Justin stepped in. "We met at a Metropolitan Bank event a few weeks ago."

"And now you're in London?" Lydia said, extending a hand to shake Mikaela's. "How do you find it so far?"

Mikaela looked at Justin's eyes narrowing. The poor asshole was panicking, wasn't he? Just the way she wanted it. "For a short vacation. I didn't even think I'd see Justin here," she said earnestly. "It's been really interesting here. I feel like five days is too short."

"Five is barely enough for this part of the city alone," Lydia told her. "Are you with friends or family?"

"Alone, actually. It's more of 'me' time," Mikaela replied. She saw a flicker of anger on Justin's face. She was pushing his temper.

"And you didn't even ring Justin for a short tour?" She looked at her son reproachfully.

"I know he's busy," Mikaela replied. "It was just a matter of huge coincidence I had to meet him here."

"Oh how lovely then. It's my daughter's engagement party today, I'd love it if you came."

"But this is a family event," Mikaela protested.

"Let's just say I'm letting a new friend in for goodwill," Lydia said with a smile. "Justin, would you be so kind to escort Mikaela to our event?"

Justin stiffly held out his arm and gave a faint, bitter look that doubled as his smile. She took it with a grin. In a matter of moments, she was introduced to the small crowd, charming almost all of them except Justin, who knew what she was up to.

Mikaela immediately found herself liking his sisters, two young women who were equally attractive and kind like their mother. She wondered why Justin had a cruel streak in him when his family was genuinely nice from her first impression of them. She wished she had brought along her camera, but figured she would look too invasive. The engagement party set-up and even the food looked like it came straight from a magazine. There was only one photographer allowed and two videographers to film the whole event, which lasted until eleven in the morning.

She was even introduced to his grand-aunt, the oldest person in the room, whose vision was still as sharp as her brain. Mikaela took this time to try to get to know Justin better, as the dame Victoria was quite talkative.

"So are you a model in America?" Victoria asked.

Mikaela laughed and shook her head. "Unfortunately, no."

"Good, because my grand nephew's been dating models, none that we've liked so far, but they're apparently liked online so much. Why, my Instagram's only got a few hundred followers but they've got more than a hundred thousand for posting bum photos."

Mikaela laughed outright, delighting the octogenarian. At least this one showed actual enthusiasm for her stories.

"Justin doesn't have Instagram or Facebook."

"With good reason. He's probably tired of all that attention."

"For a CEO, he sure gets followed around a lot by media," Mikaela said, dropping her voice.

"Oh, it all started in uni, when he dated the illegitimate daughter of one of those European royals," Victoria said. "The media liked that girl, but they found out he was interesting and poised to become an heir to one of the largest companies in the world," she relayed, taking a single grape from a fruit and cheese platter.

"What happened?"

"It lasted until the end of summer, then—" Victoria stopped.

Then what? Mikaela looked at the old woman with expectation. Then Victoria's eyes bulged out and her hands flew to her throat.

"Aunt Vicky!" Louisa cried out.

The room fell silent, and everyone was wondering what was going on with Louisa's distressed voice. Then they realized what was wrong. She was choking!

"She's choking!" someone gasped.

Justin bolted from across the room, wanting to do something but unsure of what to do. Mikaela looked in horror and her body rushed into adrenaline mode as she went behind Victoria and administered a Heimlich maneuver she had read about but had never actually done. She pulled Victoria's abdomen inward, and then upward, amid the gasps of the guests. Seconds later, a grape fell on the table and rolled all the way to the floor. Mikaela was shaking from what had happened, as the Lydia and Justin helped Victoria sit down.

Mikaela sat down across Victoria who was still trying to catch her breath, her fingers cold and her breathing shallow. Good god, had she just saved someone's life? The hotel doctor came in, along with a nurse, moments later to check on her.

"She saved my life," Victoria murmured, looking at Mikaela in awe as she allowed herself to be escorted for further checkup at the clinic. Lydia followed suit.

"You saved Aunt Vicky," Beatrice gasped, walking up to her.

Unexpectedly, Mikaela found herself wrapped in an embrace. One from Louise and one from Beatrice. Justin was staring at Mikaela, and it was something he never expected to happen. He couldn't have predicted this, he couldn't have known that Mikaela would end up being useful outside of the contract. But she had saved his beloved Grand Aunt's life.

He found himself looking at her like it was the first time he had actually seen her. Despite her unsteady hands and pallor, a byproduct of the adrenaline rush, he had found Mikaela at her most beautiful.

Chapter11

Her last day in London had been magical, by all aspects. Lydia and her daughters outdid themselves in letting Mikaela experience what remained of the city she hadn't seen yet. They were with her the whole day, shopping, having tea, and walking around.

She had dropped by Victoria's home before the hotel car drove her off to the airport. She had only seen Justin that morning, as he dropped by at the hotel before work, telling her that she would be traveling alone back to California. Her heart dropped. That was the moment she knew she was in too deep with Justin. *No one falls in love in just a few weeks*, she told herself. Even if she felt used, even if she felt like an object, she still found herself wanting him to like her back. Which was stupid. Men like Justin would never give women like her the time of the day.

Am I too nice for my own good? she wondered. *No, I can't be, I still want material things, I want to be recognized, I want sex with him…* Mikaela tried to stop the negative thoughts from forming. *I still have two more months to go*, she said to herself. *I'll get through this like how he does it. How does he do it? How can I be that cool about all of this?*

Mikaela's heart was heavy as she boarded the plane that was bringing her back to reality. He really had left her no choice. While she hadn't expected any reward, she at least expected a change of heart in him. Well, she was wrong. He hadn't even thanked her for saving his grand aunt. A vacation was still a vacation, no matter how short. Her post-vacation blues had begun the moment the plane taxied down the runway.

Nine hours of first class airplane rest, twenty pounds in excess luggage, and the gratitude of Justin's family that was beyond priceless made her feel better, if only a little while. She took a cab from the airport, giving the wrong address first (her old apartment), when her phone rang.

"Where the hell are you?" Lynne said irritated. "I was worried sick."

"I'll explain later," she said blearily.

"Are you sick?"

"No, just jetlagged," Mikaela mumbled.

"Jetlagged? Mikaela Johnson, what the hell is going on?"

"I promise I'll explain soon, maybe tomorrow. After work."

She heard Lynne sigh. "You have got a lot of talking to do, Missy."

"I'll see you then, okay?" Mikaela put down the phone and watched as the familiar streets raced by her eyes. The sun was hot, and despite her misgivings about English rain, she actually missed it.

Entering her sort of new apartment felt alien to her. It was grand, but it didn't feel welcoming. She had tried to bring some warmth to it by bringing a few of her salvaged and DIY furniture, some pictures of her family from throughout the years and even her old bedsheets. They hadn't had sex in this apartment yet, she realized. She didn't want it tainted by that ugly contract. Ugly? A vacation to London was ugly? A new apartment was ugly? She was his personal whore, at least he made it seem like she was.

Benefits were still benefits though. It was a thought she wanted to instill in herself over and over again. There was some good to come out of this. But what would her mother and father say about this?

They were dead, yes, but was she disrespecting their memory by trying to survive and enjoy life? She didn't even feel enjoyment all throughout. It was fleeting. It was torture to realize she actually liked him more than she expected she would. What was he? Another charming psychopath who just so happened to be a billionaire and whom just so happened to be one of the most gorgeous guys she'd ever met?

There was no shortage of her emotions that went like waves, up and down, and up and down. She was an idiot for allowing this to happen, to even think that he would actually look at her the way he looked at his previous girlfriends in magazines.

Yes, she had done some stalking, she had seen articles about him, and it rang in the same tone, with different bombshell women, women she could never compete with. Why the hell would she, right? He chose her, out of all the women.

Should I be flattered? Maybe I have a golden vagina, she thought almost laughing aloud to herself. She was losing her mind. Tomorrow she would have to work again, toil from seven in the morning until god knows what time, just to keep herself distracted.

She hadn't even taught the kids their dance lessons in weeks and she felt bad about it.

Justin hadn't asked her if she had safely arrived and she took it as a sign that he was only interested in her for one thing and one thing alone. She wanted to be as callous as he was, so her emotions could be at ease, so she could be at ease. She suddenly missed his mother and sisters, even if they had only been together for less than a day. She was being emotional about all of this, she was being vulnerable, showing how weak she was about finding and keeping love. Was she that needy?

She fought the urge to message him. She fought the urge to call him. Every fiber in her body wanted to talk to him, all she wanted to do was ask him how he was doing, drop a sultry hello, maybe he liked over aggressive women. Maybe he liked it if she wore sexier clothing aside from her usual loose tops and jeans. Maybe she looked too prudish for someone he wanted to keep having sex with. She could invest in lingerie. His ex-girlfriends modeled lingerie.

Mikaela thought she was desperate for his attention, which was pathetic, actually. She reached for her phone and messaged him, hoping he wasn't too busy to at least respond. She waited until she fell asleep. He never replied.

***

Her first day of work had been sluggish and her coworkers joked that she shouldn't have taken that vacation. In hindsight, there was a part of her that did regret going to London. Being there had ecstasy, excitement, and disappointment. Being back on American soil was utter disappointment. Malibu felt contained all of a sudden. She liked London for its intense diversity and bipolar weather, which was almost a match for Justin's approach toward her.

He hadn't called or texted her in a week, surely he was back, right? She saw his ticket and it said he was supposed to be back a day after she arrived. Of course, being a billionaire could mean he'd be fickle in some aspects of his life, her included.

Had he tired of her? Was he ready to pay $20,000 to get rid of her? She suddenly didn't care about the money, even if she insisted to herself that it was part of the contract. That was nursing school budget right there, some community college, some small private institution—she didn't care as long as she got to finish college. She felt anxious all the time, checked her phone often during breaks, while she showered, sometimes it was spam, and sometimes it was Lynne.

Speaking of Lynne, she hadn't told her friend the entirety of their arrangement. She just said she went to London, all expenses paid for by Justin and it was there that she saved his grand aunt from choking. Lynne wouldn't stop pestering her if they had done it or not, and she assumed because according to her, Mikaela had fallen for the billionaire playboy.

"I'm not buying the whole 'let me just get you a ticket to London because I want to' bit," Lynne said over the phone a few days ago. "There's a catch. And if you'd done it with him the way you're denying it, then there's something else in the works."

"I guess he liked my coffee."

"Or he fell for your smile," Lynne teased.

"He isn't like that. Remember our quiet date?"

"Yeah, some commoner's restaurant," Lynne joked. "Okay, so he's a boring billionaire? The tabloids made it seem like he's the bomb."

In bed he's the bomb, Mikaela thought. "Maybe he hasn't gotten over his previous girlfriend and he's taking baby steps with me."

"Baby steps? You call that baby steps? Being flown to London like you won some raffle? You make it seem like Henry will make me live on food stamps."

"How are you and Henry, anyway?" Mikaela asked, swiftly changing the subject.

Thankfully, Lynne prattled on about how her dates had been going with him, and how she thought he might be the one. He likes kids, Lynne shared.

Did Justin like kids? Mikaela realized there was a lot she didn't know about him even if they had slept together multiple times. She didn't know his favorite color, his favorite food. His favorite coffee could be the one she made for him the first day they met. Justin probably disliked hip-hop music and dancing. Or maybe he was a good singer. That was what was lacking in their relationship.

Relationship? What relationship? she reminded herself. This was purely a sexual one. The whole arrangement made her his personal ho. She shook her head and continued to listen to Lynne until her phone began to overheat on her ear and she apologetically had to end the call.

Just as she brushed her teeth, her phone rang. Panicking, she spat out the foam in her mouth and answered it.

"Hello?" she said, trying to sound as casual as possible.

"Where are you?" he asked in his usual deep-throated voice.

"At the apartment."

"I'm coming over," he said.

Just like that. Maybe he missed her, maybe he was horny. She didn't care if it was for both reasons as long as he wanted her in his life tonight. She was glad she had showered and she excitedly put on her new satin sleepwear as soon as he ended the call.

He arrived within twenty minutes.

"How was your flight?" she asked him as he walked in.

So much for small talk. He barely looked at her.

"It was okay. I was back last Tuesday," he replied.

Four days ago and he didn't even bother to pop in and say hi or have sex with her while she was asleep, huh? "Great," she lamely said.

"Is that new?" he asked her, motioning for her to go to the bedroom.

"Yeah."

"Excellent."

What? Excellent? That was it? But it was a compliment. Or was it? She didn't know how to feel about it, and she forced herself to pretend her self-esteem hadn't ebbed one bit.

Justin was in a foul mood. A few things had gone wrong in the past four days and he lost a few million, the millions didn't matter, but his ego was bruised. He hadn't focused well on work ever since Mikaela left London the previous week.

He didn't say anything as he stripped out of his shirt and his jeans. He was already hard, Mikaela saw this. He walked for her and began to kiss her, caressing her back. The kisses weren't rough this time. Her body began to grow warm, she was melting because of a mere kiss and touch.

Her nipples grew erect and he tried to contain his excitement. Justin actually wanted to take her immediately, he had been starved of sex for more than a week. He had touched her only once in London. She had to be horny, she had to cum tonight. The silk negligee she wore instantly sprang him into lust.

Trailing a hand up to her thigh, Mikaela bit her lower lip, loving how tender and warm his touch was. Her hands were curled up on his chest as he gave her another open-mouthed kiss, his tongue exploring her. He trailed his tongue down to her lower lip and he bit it gently.

He wanted her to cum tonight; it was a gratification he wanted. He slipped off one strap and her breast fell out and he held onto it, gritting his teeth. She moaned quietly, closing her eyes from the grip. He pushed her on the bed and she squirmed a little, adjusting herself. He paid no attention to her discomfort.

He held her, played with her, enjoying that she was wet.

"You miss this, don't you?" he asked her.

She said nothing, closing her eyes again, controlling herself from moaning. He enjoyed seeing her like this, helpless to lust for him. She sucked in a breath, the moment he played with her clit.

"You like that?" he asked her.

She nodded, there was nothing left to say. She hella enjoyed it, she only thought she didn't want this anymore. He stroked her gently, stroked her slowly, and she arched on the bed. As greedy as it sounded, she wanted more. It was addictive, this pleasure he was giving to her.

The strap on the other side fell off, and he took a deep breath, seeing her breasts spill out completely. He wanted to ravage her and he grew harder. She stopped him from pleasuring her some more. It was her turn.

He looked surprised as she mounted on top of him, gyrating her hips to his hips, feeling his cock quiver with excitement. She held onto him and slowly slid himself into her. He let out a quiet moan, one he didn't expect to happen. Her rhythm picked up, and Justin found himself moaning in pleasure.

He didn't want to cum just yet, but the friction she created was becoming too much. He straddled her and switched positions, easily overpowering her and she couldn't help but laugh as she landed on the bed again.

"I want you to cum," he told her, trailing kisses down her neck, enjoying her cat-like grin and hearing her laugh.

What did he just say? Was he being considerate now? He stopped her trail of thought as he pushed himself into her, slowly. He was deliberately playing with her clit, the way he rubbed himself against her. Her hips moved in unison and he groaned again, feeling the tightness envelop him.

Mikaela felt this was different tonight, different from all the others. He was taking his sweet time, building up sensations she never thought existed. She flung her legs over his back, and she continued rocking her hips against him. She was so wet, he thought it would drive him crazy if he didn't cum tonight. The heat between them was becoming unbearable. Her fingers dug on his back as he controlled his motion.

He found his pace picking up, thrusting faster and deeper into him, hearing her moan louder and she arched her back to meet him. He let out a groan, entering into her harder. The little motions she was making drove him nuts. He bent down to grate his teeth against her breasts and she found herself whimpering. As she continued moving her hips, he moaned louder this time, unable to control it. She hadn't cum yet.

He slipped out of her and slid down to lick her. He felt the tangy taste of her, her female scent and he licked her slowly, tracing the outline of her lips. She shuddered and he didn't stop licking her. Her tender flesh throbbed and she writhed as he teased her, sucking her juices. She was engorged and throbbing, in need of him inside her. She moaned louder, she screamed a little. He slipped into her again, pounding harder and harder.

It was so good, she came twice.

*

Chapter12

She woke up, dazed, wondering what time it was. It was barely three in the morning. She shifted and felt someone beside her. It was Justin. He was fast asleep beside her. This had never happened. He always left as soon as he was satisfied with the sex. Maybe he wasn't satisfied? Was that why he was still here? She didn't want to stare at him, but she couldn't help it.

He looked vulnerable while asleep, and she just had to smile. His naked body was perfect and she wanted to remember him all unguarded like this. She saw him frown a little and she looked away, pretending to be asleep. She heard him shifting on the bed, trying to make as little noise as possible. She heard shuffling from his side and she braced herself to pretend it was going to be fine the moment he'd step out of bed, the moment the door would screech to a close.

There was minimal movement at first, and she continued to close her eyes, pretending she was oblivious to what he was about to do. She felt him move out of bed, shuffling about for his clothes. She heard him put them on, she heard him put his shoes on. She closed her eyes tightly, hating the feeling that was overcoming her. She felt abandoned, she felt used again, she felt—

A kiss on her cheek, a very light one.

She almost opened her eyes in shock, but she waited until he had left her bedroom, waited until she heard the main door close before she did. She bolted up from bed, sitting down, looking at that slice of light from underneath the door. Did he actually kiss her? He actually kissed her! He kissed her. She didn't care if it was on the cheek. Were her efforts being rewarded? Was this thanks for saving his grand aunt? Maybe, just maybe he was beginning to feel things for her.

Could she assume this was true? Was it really happening? She smiled to herself, hugging her pillow.

She couldn't sleep the rest of the night, tormented and excited about hundreds of things running through her head. One thing was for sure however, she wanted to see him tomorrow. And the day after that. And the day after that.

***

He drove home past three in the morning, he had waited until she was fast asleep to leave. That was the most respectful thing he could do. He hadn't been very nice to her lately, but he didn't really want to see her until his manly urges became too strong. She had that magnetic quality about her, he guessed. Her pull was greater than the other women he had dated before.

The moment he found out she had boarded that flight, he resisted the urge to send a message, asking her to take care of herself. He ended up rewriting it three times since he kept deleting it. In the end he chose not to send it. Here he was, filled with sentiment for her, all because she saved his grand aunt Vicky from choking. Or was that the reason?

Her attempts at trying to catch his attention failed miserably. He felt like he was looking at some high schooler, haphazardly doing her best to be noticed by him. His ego had inflated momentarily, but it deflated a bit when she denied him of sex in her hotel room. He had never been denied of sex before and he had wanted it so terribly, he vented out his frustrations to staff with every small infraction that he never bothered with before.

He told himself he was probably overwhelmed that Beatrice was now formally engaged. British Tabloids kept releasing photos for days. There were a few articles on his grand aunt choking and being saved by an attending guest. He breathed in relief to know there were no photos of that incident or her.

He waited until the sun rose across the horizon, a first in many years. The last time he waited for it was a few weeks after his father's death and he had been sitting in the same spot, in the same couch, alone in his thoughts.

This was a repeat of that. It was something significant then. *I'm just thankful*, he told himself again and again. He was making a big deal out of a tiny peck on the cheek, something she wouldn't even have felt. It was the last thing he wanted, to be bothered by a person who didn't mean much to his life, a person who couldn't give him something in return, aside from being bound by the contract. There was a slight regret to his thoughts.

I never regret, he thought savagely.

An hour after Mikaela boarded that flight back to California, Louisa called him up while he was in the midst of making a civil, yet angry email.

"Yes?" he said curtly.

"Bad day?" Louisa began.

"Yes."

"We had Mikaela dropped off at the airport earlier."

"Oh, thanks," he said distractedly.

"I like her," she pressed on.

"I'm sure you do. We all do. She did help Aunt Vicky."

"Help? She saved Aunt Vicky."

"Same thing. Where are you off to, now?"

"Oh, I'm waiting for Beatrice at the designer's studio. She's getting her dress drawn today or something. I told her to get something off the web but she wouldn't hear of it."

Justin found himself laughing. It wasn't like they couldn't afford a wedding gown. Hell, his budget for this wedding was sky's the limit, even if he knew the Murray family would commit to half of the expenses. He just didn't want them to. He had however, successfully persuaded Beatrice into making a prenup agreement.

"Let her be, it's her wedding. Just wait for yours, then you can demand for what you want," he told her.

"Justin, you don't want her to get married, do you?" she suddenly said.

"Who told you that? Have you been eavesdropping on me and Mum again?"

"No!" she said in a shrill voice. "It just seems like it. I know you think she's too young."

"Of course she is. She hasn't even finished uni."

"She really is in love, and I hope I find someone who loves me the way Gregory loves Bea," Louisa admitted.

He rolled his eyes a little but smiled. It was amusing to hear about his sister's feelings. She was a romantic one, in fact all the women in his family was. Hell, his father wasn't shy to show how he loved his wife, showering her with attention, kisses and embraces, gifts and vacations.

It was a love he had thought was ideal, something he couldn't have with the women he was dating. There was a reason why he had never found the ideal woman. She was too ideal, some fantasy he hadn't grasped yet. Perhaps Mikaela was the closest one to being ideal, but she was a far cry from all the women he had previously dated. She wasn't cultured, she didn't have connections, she barely had any sense of fashion until she met him and he brusquely commented on her style.

"You'll find someone, Lou," he told her.

"And you?" she teased.

"Not my time yet."

"Because the tabloids say so?"

"Are you pressuring me to stay in a stable relationship right now?"

"No, but Mum isn't getting any younger."

"Please don't remind me. Mum still looks fabulous for her age."

"Honestly, Justin. We'd think you'd have settled down by now."

"You called me to lecture me, your older brother, to get into a committed relationship? That doesn't scream sibling love, you know."

"Well, we thought Mikaela Johnson was perfect."

"No one is perfect," he reminded her.

"'Cause you're the only one that is?"

"I didn't say that. Lou, I have to work."

"No you don't. Mum wants to have some tea with you later before you leave."

"I'm extending my stay so we can have tea for the next four days to her heart's content."

"Mum also told me you could invite Mikaela back, and she could stay at the house."

"Are you Mum's postmaster now?"

"She just told me to tell you that. Come on, Jus, I'm bored here. They haven't even begun designing my gown yet, or Mum's."

"Then bugger off, bother someone else, will you?"

Louisa gave a laugh from the other end. "Jus, really, lighten up. You weren't this serious before. It's like you've got a stick up your arse."

"I'll have this checked at the hospital later," he replied. They both laughed.

It was clear his mother had taken a such a strong liking to Mikaela that Louisa had to mention her name a couple of times. Louisa was beginning to show signs of it, too. That wasn't such a good thing for his position and hers.

Mikaela was a likeable person, but she just wasn't fit for him. They were only compatible with sex. It was all he thought of when he thought of her. Perhaps he was a sex addict and he didn't know it yet. But if he was, he didn't need to stick with her, right? He could have found countless others, ready to strip naked and jump into bed with him. Mikaela was no different.

He saw how she approved of his physical features at the bank event. She was so eager for him, she even changed the way she dressed, she had become more chic, in an effort to please him, and the satin lingerie she wore earlier was the stuff made out of adolescent dreams.

He recalled her herculean efforts when she saved Aunt Vicky. No one was quick enough, except her. She was on the right track, wanting to be a nurse, then maybe a doctor if she wanted to. He thought about extending the corporation's social responsibility to education. She deserved to finish her studies. He thought about helping her with her tuition. Justin had never had a problem with his and his siblings' educational expenses. Mikaela was one of those rare people who worked hard and saved a lot for studies.

No matter how stressful her day was, she tried to smile. He saw this as he passed by the café one day, without her knowledge. From inside his car, he saw her close the café, dancing and singing to some hip-hop song by the way she moved. It made him smile, seeing how upbeat she still was, along with two other co-workers who enjoyed her closing performance. There was something about her smile. *Lots of people have nice smiles*, he told himself, but her smile was a stunner, however.

She had that beguiling, wide smile that many would want to see. He had sort of expected to see that kind of smile grace the covers of magazines, billboards, and maybe on those pesky online ads that popped up so often. It was surprising to find a face like that in a coffee shop, how could the model scouts have missed that? She didn't need to be tall, she could have been a face model…

No, she shouldn't be a model. There was a reason why he picked her, she was different from all the other women he had met. There was some kindness in her that radiated, and frankly, it annoyed him, because he couldn't be as kind as she was. That was probably why he liked to tease her, so he couldn't see her smile. It made him think otherwise. It made him vulnerable if he responded to her…

Now, in front of the California sunrise, he found himself stripping out of his clothes and quickly putting on his wetsuit, one he hadn't used in months, since his father's death anniversary. Then he took out his surfboard and paddled out to sea.

***

She wanted to see him, but it never happened. He didn't answer her calls or texts. It had been five days and she was getting antsy once more. Perhaps he flew off to London again? He was a busy man, after all. She read somewhere that one could never be successful in juggling work and relationships. One always had to give way to the other. She He saw how he loved his family, though. He seemed more relaxed with them.

Maybe he was teaching her a delayed lesson for refusing to have a good romp with him back in London. She had gotten that lingerie set just to tease him. Thoughts about Justin were affecting her so much that she began to lose sleep. She began to forget things, she smiled less. This was noticed by the owner, who promptly called her to his office to have a nice little employer to employee chat.

"All right, what's going on?" he began. "You've been acting all weird since your vacation. Where'd you go, anyway?"

"Washington," she lied, unable to believe she lied. She felt bad, but she didn't want to say she went on an international trip and that she stayed in a five-star boutique hotel. She would resign on her own terms.

"Washington? That isn't even worthy of a vacation. I was expecting Hawaii or something. Maybe abroad."

"I can't afford that. I was there to-to see my parents and my brother. I haven't visited in a while…" her voice trailed off.

The owner stopped. So she was there to visit her family's graves. He felt a pang of sympathy for her and he nodded. "I hope it hasn't affected you too much. You deserved a good vacation, not a weepy one."

"I had fun. It was a mix of feelings, actually," she told him, remembering parts of her London trip. Sure, there were enjoyable times, but there had been moments she felt like crying. *Keep it all in, sucker*, she told herself. She wouldn't allow herself to cry in front of her boss, either.

"Can you hang on for the day?"

"I can hang on till next year," she replied with a smile.

"'Atta girl."

She left the office with a smile on her face, but there was a part of her that wanted to scream. A part of her that wanted to run up to Justin and slap him until he came to his senses. She wanted to shout at him, tell him she wasn't difficult to love, that she already liked him too much to back out. She told herself she wasn't in love yet, or maybe she was in love, and the length of time she had known him made her conscious about it.

There were many factors she shouldn't like him. He was arrogant, conceited, and though he treated women like royalty, there was just no warmth there, he almost had no sense of kindness. Money and power, and maybe his inflated ego ruled his world. There was no room in that kind of world for her. Yet, here she was, pining over someone who would never look at her the way she looked at him.

How could he ignore her for five days? As soon as she got home, she texted him, asking how he was. It was past seven when she got home, and she thought he would be home by then. The minutes seemed like hours as she waited for a reply. He didn't reply again. It was getting embarrassing for her, but she swallowed her pride.

If you want something, you have to work for it, she thought. She was no man-eater, but she told herself she wasn't ugly enough to keep guys away. She had thought she had used her smile to her advantage, but he was cold and heartless. It was the first time her smile hadn't worked on someone. It stung her pride a little, actually.

She had finished showering when she saw her phone blink. She quickly grabbed it, almost losing grip of her phone. It was Justin. She smiled.

I'm fine.

That was all he said. He didn't even bother to ask how she was doing. She suddenly wanted revenge again. He was doing this on purpose. He was a frickin' sadist. Did she just think about the word frickin', instead of a curse word? What was happening to her? She wasn't cursing when an opportune time to curse was now.

And he wasn't even in the same room with her. She couldn't bring herself to say one curse word anymore. He had changed that part of her, and she didn't know if she was happy about it or not. Cursing was part of her spontaneity, something she picked up after her parents died, a coping mechanism.

That's great. What are you up to tonight? she asked him.

Sleep, probably.

She stopped herself from replying. It was clear he wasn't in a conversational mood. She carelessly tossed her phone away.

Tomorrow, she would teach the kids at the center. That could take her mind off things. She still hung onto some strange notion that he would really end up liking her.

She hated the feeling.

Chapter 13

Strangely enough, the day after she stopped texting him, he called her, while she was on lunch break.

"What do you want?" she asked curtly.

"Did you enroll at nursing school already?"

"No," she said, surprised he asked.

"Great, I saw a scholarship you might like."

"Scholarship?" she repeated. "I'm twenty-four years old, way past a scholarship."

"It's a medical scholarship. Until twenty-five years of age," he said. "You'll have to move out of Malibu, though."

"Where?" she asked, forgetting about the whole plan to get annoyed at him.

"Santa Barbara."

"I can't," she quickly said. "Living there is too expensive."

"The scholarship is a good one, though. And if you have a great scholastic record, you could apply." He knew she had a good scholastic record, which was part of his private investigator's report.

She felt he was pushing her away though, but she didn't comment on that. "I'll think about it," she said, wanting to end the call all of a sudden. He didn't ask her how she was, but he thought about her the moment he heard about the scholarship through one of his acquaintances, who was chairman of the board for that certain prestigious school.

He heard the tiredness in her voice. She sounded disinterested. Was she giving up on her nursing dreams? He disliked the idea that she would be that weak, that undetermined to give up on continuing her education.

"You okay there?" he asked, before she could end the call.

"Just tired," she said.

"Would you like to have dinner later?" he asked her. "I'll pick you up."

"Where?" she said, startled that he asked that. "Didn't you want this low key?"

"At my beach house," he said. "It's still low key."

His place. His place was reserved for family and family alone. Maybe ex-girlfriends and a few friends. He had asked someone for dinner in the privacy of his house. Mikaela was merely a contract, but he had said this one impulse. He wondered what overcame him. What was going on with him? He couldn't take it back, though. He wondered what he was going to cook for her already...

"Sure," she replied, after a pregnant pause.

He almost sighed in relief that she said yes. He didn't want to be turned down. That had happened only twice in his life and he never saw those women again, even if they begged for him to date them. *No one refuses me*, he had thought. He ended the call first, still wondering why he said that. He could have said that they could have dinner at her place, or at the penthouse, but no, he just had to say that.

On the other end, Mikaela felt hope flutter again. He was asking her out on a date. A real date, at his own place. She tried to contain her excitement, and managed to sound nonchalant until the call ended. She was more excited about the dinner date than news of a scholarship. It wasn't feasible anyway, moving to Santa Monica.

This went beyond the contract. That left room for emotional attachment, a lot of room for it. Suddenly, she was half-anxious about what could happen. They had sex, they both fell asleep, and he kissed her goodbye… Would it happen again? Her mind raced. What would she wear? It was just going to be a house, but she wanted to look made up, although not too made up. She looked at the clock and saw she had five more hours of work to go. She couldn't wait till she punched out.

"I see you're busy," Mary Ann remarked, raising an eyebrow.

"Oh, I just ate," Mikaela stammered.

"Half a sandwich?"

"Not too hungry," Mikaela smiled, feeling her mood elevate. "Your turn to eat."

Mary Ann shook her head and smiled. That guy with the fancy car must've been persistent. She hadn't seen Mikaela this giddy in months. Even if she tried to hide it. Mikaela wasn't exactly easy to read, but it was her smile that made things easier to notice. That coy smile when she put down her phone said it all.

Mikaela worked steadily and surprised her coworkers when she left fifteen minutes after her shift ended. She didn't linger to help some more, or cover for someone else who wanted to take a break.

"Where's she off to?" someone asked Mary Ann.

"A date, I guess," Mary Ann said with a smile.

***

Mikaela chose denim shorts and a tank top. It looked very casual, but she thought it would suit the date. It wasn't a formal date and for that she was glad. She did some light makeup, best that she could do, because Lynne wasn't here. Besides, who needed makeup when you were in someone's house and it was beside the beach?

She wondered what it was like. She expected it to be big, though, big and lonely. It seemed he didn't like anyone around him too much.

She had quickly canceled the dance practice with the kids, hoping her friend would cover for her. She felt bad she had canceled when she hadn't taught in weeks, but her personal life was at stake here, too.

Her doorbell rang and he walked in. "Hi," he said casually.

"Hi," she said, noticing she felt shy, like this was their first date. It wasn't but it felt like it had been a long time. She wanted to kick herself for being childish. This was still his way of wanting to sleep with her, except he was being nicer this time.

"Ready to go?" he asked her. "Don't forget to bring a sweater just in case."

She nodded. "Have one in my bag."

"Excellent."

He had brought along a top-down Mercedes, and her eyes widened, seeing how sleek it was. Then she realized people around them were staring at the car. Again. He was an easy target for hooligans if she still stayed in her old neighborhood. As soon as he started the car, the roof retracted and she slid into the passenger seat, feeling the luxurious handmade leather upholstery underneath her palms.

Some billboard song was playing on the touchscreen radio system, a tune that made her want to dance.

"You dance?" he asked her as he drove away from the condominium.

She nodded. "I teach hip-hop dance at a kid's clinic."

"How do you find time for that?"

"My days off, if it falls on the weekend."

He didn't know about that, that she taught dance to kids. "Do you get paid for that?"

"Hell, no," she stopped, seeing the look on his face. "No. I'd like to think of it as giving back to the community."

"Are these street kids or something? Orphans?"

She shook her head. "No, they're just kids who live close to the coffee shop. They saw me dancing before, but that dance studio closed down. It was my way of exercising."

So that explained her figure. She was curvy in all the right places and she was lithe in bed… He took a breath, controlling his lust. "That's really nice of you."

"Thanks," she replied, not looking at him.

"Did you always like dancing?"

She smiled wistfully. "Since I could remember. Mom and Dad loved jazz dance. Jazz music, basically classic Hollywood."

Justin remembered the posters in her previous apartment. She liked classic movies, which he found strange. He hadn't bothered to ask, he just thought it was a mismatch against her personality. He had seen her current apartment, and while her own things looked unkempt, the things he had gotten for her remained neat. He had finally seen more photos of her family in that quick visit to her apartment. She looked exactly like her mother, those were some good genes. They arrived twenty minutes after an easy drive, a cooler breeze flipping through her hair.

She couldn't see much of the house yet. Just a whitewashed wall with an automatic gate in a wooden finish. Was it going to be as stark as his penthouse? As soon as the gates slid open, her eyes popped out.

This was his house? It was probably the biggest house she had ever seen. From the entrance, she could see the coastline, with some boats and their lights like fireflies in the sea. She heard the wave after wave crash on the shore, high tide was coming. She gingerly took a first step, as if afraid she would mess up the floor.

He smiled at her. "Come on. This way."

He led her into the dining area with its open plan, adjacent to the common living room area, which had its own billiards table. She found herself walking straight for the balcony, staring in awe at the infinity-edged swimming pool with its glass walls for security. Beyond that was a series of steps that led to the beach. It looked like heaven in Malibu.

"You live here alone?" she asked him.

"Most of the time," he admitted.

"How many bedrooms are there?"

"Six. Not counting the movie room and the gym."

"How can you have so many houses?" she asked, walking closer to the pool.

"I don't. It's the company's," he said.

"The company is yours."

"This was my dad's favorite vacation house."

"Was?"

"He's... He passed away years ago."

"Oh." Her tone changed. "I'm sorry."

He shrugged. "It's okay. That was years ago. Anyway, what do you want to have for dinner? I've narrowed it down to pasta and hamburgers and fries."

"Pasta sounds faster," she said.

He nodded. "Pasta it is."

They walked back into the kitchen, with Mikaela still looking around the place. Everything screamed designer in the house. Why the hell would anyone want designer brand pillowcases?

He saw the look on her face. "You can walk around, you know. This place only has two floors. Go on," he prodded.

"I can?"

"Yeah." He knew she wouldn't steal anything, remembering her looking around for him in the penthouse. It was something he had taken into consideration, which was why he put the $1,000 there just in case she got the greedy eye.

He heard Mikaela's footsteps on the hardwood floors his father had exported from Malaysia, and he smiled. He had never invited anyone that wasn't his girlfriend to this place. It was too personal for him, even if his sisters held summer parties here once in a while, he considered this house a little escapade from the pressures that life so willingly gave to him. Mikaela got back down after ten minutes, as soon as he had drained the pasta and rinsed it in cold, running water.

"I didn't know you could cook," she commented.

"There are a lot of things you don't know about me," he said.

"That's because you don't talk much. It's not part of the contract," Mikaela told him.

"Try me."

She blinked. "All right," she said, looking up at the ceiling. "When's your birthday?"

"The day before we met."

"I didn't get to greet you." She sounded disappointed.

"I didn't throw a party, I just stayed at home. Talked to my family."

"That was it? I expected something more spectacular, a grand house party filled with booze and women."

He huffed. "What have you been reading? Media likes to sensationalize. Why do you think they've survived for so long?"

"Whatever is newsworthy?"

"Yes, whatever is newsworthy. Like dating models and celebrities and whatnot. Half is true, half is exaggerated, and majority of it is false. I happen to like my quiet time."

"What happened to your last girlfriend?" she suddenly asked as he deftly added olive oil to sundried tomatoes.

He shook the pan around, then he looked up. "She and I ended on bad terms."

"You're actually answering my questions tonight."

"I'm feeling pretty magnanimous."

"Deep word, but I feel like it means you'd like to share."

"Bingo."

"How bad was it?"

"She was jealous about everything. Jealous about the attention I gave my mother and sisters."

Mikaela couldn't help but make a face. That was just plain weird. Family was everything, she knew this because she had none. "You couldn't talk her out of it?"

"That was who she was, and we had to part ways."

"Where is she now?"

"You've seen her around. She's the new Hawaiian Tropics model."

"Her," Mikaela breathed out. That model's legs were a million miles long. She was gorgeously blonde and tan, she had to admit.

"See, you know her."

"So you like models better?"

"Easy access," he shrugged.

Her eyes narrowed. Well, at least she wasn't a model. And he was suddenly harsh, but he was tactless like that, she had nearly forgotten. "How come your sisters didn't attend college here?"

He smiled as he dumped the pasta into the pan, drizzling it with olive oil again. "They love the beaches here, but prefer the educational system there."

"How is your Aunt Vicky, by the way?" she interrupted him.

"She's doing okay. She did message me, told me to say hello to you."

"She did?" Mikaela smiled, happy she had been remembered.

He looked at her. "You look like you won a million dollars or something."

"It's nice to know I'm remembered."

"Who would forget you?" he told her. "Aunt Vicky almost died and you expect her to forget you?"

"Well," she shrugged, trying to find the right words to say without sounding needy. "Everyone was busy that day and she found the time to talk to me."

"Because you gate-crashed?" he teased.

"Did I really?"

"You partially did that on purpose," he said with an all-knowing smile. "You're quite easy to read."

"I am not."

"Yes you are."

"Fine, a little. All right, do you do any sports?" she asked as he took out black ceramic plates. She was glad she wore shorts, seeing it was a very casual date. They were eating by the kitchen on high stools and she liked it a lot.

He nodded. "A few. Used to play lacrosse at uni. I've surfed, too," he said, remembering his sojourn a few days ago.

"You surf? Wow. I guess I'm just bad at that."

"You're a dancer, you're good at dancing. I can't dance to save my life, you know."

"I can teach you."

"You can do the waltz, too?" he asked.

She nodded. "I may teach hip-hop but I know the basics of the jive, foxtrot, and the waltz."

He smiled at her as he handed her a plate with a heaping of pasta. "Hope you like this." He also took out a decanter of white wine. "This is just in case," he added and she laughed.

"Yeah, I'm sure I won't be drinking too much of that." She took her first bite and grinned at him. "This is restaurant quality."

"What kind of restaurant? Indulge me."

"Those star rated restaurants," she said, trying to look for the right term.

"Did you mean Michelin star?"

"That one!"

He laughed. "Really now? I hope you aren't pulling my leg."

"Hey I'm getting free dinner, might as well make you feel happy cooking for me."

"You're washing the dishes."

She laughed, a loud burst that sounded fun to listen to. "I don't mind. Still cheaper than dinner out."

"I have dessert too."

"Please don't tell me you make a mean cake," she said. Then he'd be too ideal. Which shouldn't happen.

"I bought it, it's my mum that makes it."

"I like it when you talk in a British accent."

"I get confused sometimes. So my accent sounds too fake to be American or too fake to be British."

"I still like it," she said, then realized she had said it so calmly it was as if she had told him she loved him. She looked down and concentrated on her pasta.

"Can I ask you something?"

"What?"

"Have you ever considered marriage?"

He shook his head. "I don't believe in divorce. If you can't work things out with simple things, better avoid marriage."

"Did your parents get divorced?"

"On the contrary," he replied, "they were together for twenty-five years. Which is why I don't believe in divorce."

"But your previous relationships were short?"

"No, my dating was short. All my relationships lasted more than six months. So that's where the tabloids get it wrong. I'm only a playboy when I'm single."

"You're single now."

"Does it bother you?"

She was quiet for a while. "I'm confused about it."

He shook his head. "Careful now."

"Yeah, I'm being careful." She finished her pasta and sipped a bit of wine. "What's your favorite color?"

He burst out chuckling. "Are you kidding me? Have we really come to this?"

"Just answer the question. You said I had to try," she insisted.

"All right, I like midnight blue."

"That's pretty specific."

"Would you like to stay on the couch? I hope you don't mind me drinking," he said.

"I don't."

They didn't sit too close to each other. They were a throw pillow distance away from touching. It was as if he didn't want to touch her tonight. This was something new to their arrangement. There was no television screen in front of the couch, which was surprising. They instead had a view of the expanse of the Malibu coast. Star shone in the sky as the waves softly hit the sand from below.

Mikaela found herself hugging a pillow as she listened to the lulling sound.

"Why don't you like it when I curse?"

"It leaves a bad impression. And that doesn't go for you alone. It sounds hostile."

"I curse because it feels good when I do."

"Where did you learn this?"

"After my parents died…"

He stopped her. "Let's not talk about that. Let's talk happy things."

Like what? The contract ending? That he would move on so easily to other women? There would be other contracts. She was just the first.

"Do you like being alone?"

"I think it beats being surrounded by a lot of people who annoy me," he replied.

"Do I annoy you?"

He looked at her like she was asking the most ridiculous thing. "Sometimes you do. You're too nice for your own good."

"I'm not. I just see the good in people."

"You shouldn't and that's unsolicited advice from a businessman."

"Not everything is business."

"Of course it is. There's an exchange for everything."

She sighed. "You mean our contract. It's almost on its third month."

"I know," he said quietly. He wanted to say something, but it seemed like word vomit.

"You don't hate me, do you?" she pressed on.

"Hate is a strong word, Mikaela."

"So that's a no?"

"Of course it's a no. Hate is debilitating in decision making. It clouds reasoning, even for people."

"So you don't hate me, but you don't like me either."

"I made a contract with you, I think that's good enough grounds for liking you."

He was answering this like a politician and it annoyed the hell out of her. She decided to be blunt with him.

"I don't like how you treat me."

"Which part of the contract did I violate?"

"You didn't. I did," she began.

"What?" he frowned, "I'm not really—"

"Justin?"

"What?"

"Shut up and kiss me."

***

She woke up with a smile on her face. The sex wasn't mind-blowing yesterday. In fact, there was no sex involved at all. After they kissed, they spend the rest of the time talking, not noticing that it was past one in the morning. She had never heard him talk the way he did last night. He was animated, as if he was talking to a dear friend, or a lover. But she was his lover, wasn't she?

Nothing was said about how she felt, but she knew he felt it. And she felt something from him as well. He was beginning to like her, wasn't he? It was finally becoming real. It was really happening to her. Her happiness overflowed as she set about for work despite lacking sleep. The way he kissed her last night was different, like their last act of lovemaking. She could call it lovemaking now, with confidence. She wondered if he was late for work too, wondered if he felt as energetic as she did because of their first real date last night.

Her work day had gone along pretty well, and she had sent in her application for that nursing scholarship in Santa Monica before she went to work. It was an impulse decision. If she and Justin ended up together, then she would manage the daily two-hour long trip just to study, and she would do it willingly.

She was getting ahead of herself, wasn't she? But she smiled while she worked, feeling that things were finally going her way, that he was beginning to reciprocate. So that cold bastard actually had emotions deep down, and she had cracked him open. She wondered if he showed that side of him to the others. It didn't matter. She was the present. She had a feeling that contract was going to change. Feelings made people change.

He hadn't texted or called her today and she wondered if he was busy again, and she felt better that he was. *He's working for our future,* she jokingly told herself. There was no shortage of giddiness today, and she found herself texting him during lunch time, asking him how his morning was. There was no response yet, but she was all right with it.

She would resign next week, to prepare herself for classes. She had a good feeling she'd be getting that scholarship. She had, in fact, written a letter to her boss already. He wouldn't be pleased, but he would be happy she was doing this for her future career. Mikaela wondered if Justin was all right with her chosen path. She was no millionaire heiress, she was no celebrity, but she worked diligently and with passion. She hoped Justin would find that enough.

She received a text at four in the afternoon.

Please check bank account.

Did he send her money again? He had sent her $2,000 last week. It was too much, even for someone who was struggling to get to school. Maybe this was his way of helping her move to Santa Monica. What a sweetheart.

What's it for? she had asked.

Just for you.

And that was it. No other pleasantries. She wondered how long this was going to last, his penchant for stiff behavior in nearly everything. She shrugged it off. There was a reason for this money, and that was to help her. She told herself she'd pay him back if he ever lent a hand with her schooling. With that thought, Mikaela continued to work happily.

The Final Chapter

A week passed by and still he didn't call or text or pop up unexpectedly. She had expected him to sweep her off on a random date, but it hadn't happened since that night. She relished and replayed that night every few hours, desperately wanting to see him again. How sad was that? She couldn't shrug it off so easily. That ugly feeling was back again. She was feeling abandoned. She had checked her bank account on whim yesterday and she saw $20,000 in it, which made her do a double-take. She hadn't had that much money since her family died.

She planned to call him today to thank him and tell him it was too much, but first things first—Lynne wanted some girl time with her. She was head over heels for her current beau, Henry Nichols.

"I know it's only been a month, but I can't help myself," Lynne gushed. "This is it, Mikaela!"

Mikaela laughed, masking her confusion over Justin pretty well. "Isn't it too soon? I don't want to see you cry for some douche."

"I won't," she said confidently. "I'm telling you he's the one," she insisted, squeezing Mikaela's arm.

"Ow, stop it."

Lynne quickly let go and grinned broadly as they walked down, headed for the beach in their shorts, bikinis and lace tops. They hadn't had sun in a while and Mikaela was glad Lynne was there to take some worries out of her mind.

They had begun to walk on the sidewalk, where numerous food stands and coffee shops were, along with a few tabloid and newspaper stands when Mikaela stopped, seeing something familiar. She walked closer to the magazine stand and grabbed a newspaper.

"Hey, no free reading," the man said.

Mikaela distractedly shoved coins into his hand, not bothering to count how much she actually gave. It was a sleazy tabloid with Justin's face on it and beside him was another woman in a bikini. It looked like it was shot outside of his home.

She read through the small article with ten large pictures of him lying beside her on the sand. There were more photos of him putting suntan lotion on her bare back, of him kissing her shoulder, of him smiling, a rare and large smile. She was a model, no doubt about it, with her figure and tan. Mikaela hadn't realized her hands were shaking and Lynne was watching her very much worried.

"Mikaela?" she began, reaching out for her.

Mikaela's eyes were as wide as saucers, racing through the article.

Playboy Billionaire Justin Henderson Dating Again (And This Time it's with Vida Karlovac) screamed the headline and sub headline.

Was this for real? Maybe this was an old newspaper. It couldn't be recent. They had only had dinner six days ago. He shared things with her, they had fun together, and he cooked for her and kissed her in a way that all women wanted to be kissed…

No, no, no, she thought over and over again. She blinked and closed her eyes and saw the date. It was taken last Saturday, that day she waited for him to reply. That day he had told her to check her bank account. It couldn't be. He wouldn't dare. Then she remembered the contract.

"I'll add this to the contract, then," he said. "For good measure. If I ever cheat on you, I'll give you twenty thousand. How does that sound?"

It dawned on Mikaela that he had sent that money so he would keep to the agreement. So he had cheated on her! She had lost and won at the same time. It was a horrible feeling and she found herself on the verge of tears.

Lynne grabbed the paper from her, seeing Mikaela's face in distress. She paused, seeing the photos, very incriminating photos of Mikaela's supposed date. "Oh sweetie," she murmured.

Mikaela quickly grabbed the paper again from Lynne's hands and looked over the article again.

"Stop it," Lynne told her. "Give that to me."

"Is this for real?" Mikaela whispered, trying to make some sense of everything.

She had assumed too much; she had hoped for too much. She didn't tell Lynne everything, the whole contract. All she said was they were seeing each other and that they had had intimate moments. It was obviously enough, since Lynne went overprotective and empathetic on her/

"Give me that newspaper," Lynne demanded, pulling her closer. "Don't cry, not here."

Mikaela nodded and followed Lynne, who held her hand as they walked their way to Lynne's car. It took all her strength to stop the waterworks, but once she got inside the car, the dam broke and tears flooded her face.

"Shit," Mikaela muttered.

Lynne sat across her on the driver's side. "He doesn't deserve you."

Mikaela shook her head. "No one deserves him. He's an asshole."

"That's right!"

"But I love that asshole," Mikaela sniffed.

Lynne gave a deep sigh. "Well, that's not good for you." So it had come to this, her friend had finally fallen in love with a man who had a reputation for changing women as fast as he changed his suits.

"I should have known,"

"But you didn't."

"I know, why didn't I? The signs were all over. No, it was obvious from the start."

"I'm sorry I pushed you into dating him."

"No." Mikaela shook her head. "That was my choice. And it wasn't a smart one. I might have enjoyed that trip to London, might have enjoyed perks I've never had before, but I've never felt this miserable since-since..."

"Don't say anything about your family," Lynne told her firmly. "You're smart, you're pretty, and you work hard. You don't need a guy like that in your life."

"No, no, you don't understand—"

"You love him and you can't see your way out of this?" Lynne told her mildly. "Of course you can. Remember that horrible ex of yours? He cheated on you and yet you moved on well."

"This is different."

"What? He's got a big dick and a ton of money? Big deal. What's he got that others don't?"

Mikaela was quiet for a moment as she dried her tears. That wasn't a good way to react. It only showed how deep into it she was. She suddenly wanted to laugh at what Lynne just said. She also wanted to continue crying. It was all so stupid. She was stupid. She had a feeling this would happen. She told herself time and time again things would work in her favor, and yet, she had doubts. Those doubts had come to life. He had replaced her so easily, like how he gave away money so easily.

Her life had revolved around him the moment she signed the contract. She had given away her pride, her kindness and her freedom, all for him. All for some ungrateful, demented— she stopped herself, wanting to throw up from the enormity of what happened.

Did it really feel like this? When you loved someone so much and you found out they cheated on you? She never thought it would hurt this much, she didn't even cry when her last ex-boyfriend cheated on her. Justin, he was different. She was too in love with him, she didn't even feel the need to murder him, but she wanted to shoot herself for being so weak.

This is what you get for not being careful enough. He warned you again and again, and you still wanted to get his attention, you still wanted him to at least like you. You are such an idiot, Mikaela Johnson!

She had already resigned from work, and planned her move to Santa Monica. She'd thought he would be there, be by her side to support her all the way. She should have listened to that voice in her head that said this was all a bad idea. A bad idea? Falling in love? How could that be a bad idea? Because she wanted him to love her back?

No one falls in love after the first date, she told herself. She certainly didn't. But their first real dinner date sealed the deal. She had fallen for his wiles, she had fallen for his charm, and his psychopathic tendencies had worked on her even if she had battled herself on this. She had allowed herself to be manipulated because she was blinded by him, by his looks, by his dashing character, by the material things he showered her with, and no matter how unkind he was to her, she found herself wanting him to like her even more.

Plus, he had kissed her! He had kissed her while he thought she was asleep. Didn't that speak in volumes? Didn't that mean something?

She felt something there, some shred of affection, some expression of warmth. It must have meant nothing to him. Or maybe it was a goodbye, the kindest farewell he could muster.

Whatever his reasons were, it left Mikaela wretched. It left her bruised all over, it left her fatigued. She had let the contract get to her.

Full discretion must be maintained, the contract said.

He didn't really want her seen anywhere. She was just kidding herself, she was stupid, so very stupid to even think he would look at her twice. Now look where it landed her, some guy made an idiot out of her, and the worst thing was she allowed it to happen.

"All my relationships lasted more than six months. So that's where the tabloids get it wrong. I'm only a playboy when I'm single," he told her.

"You're single now," she said.

"Does it bother you?"

She was quiet for a while. "I'm confused about it."

He shook his head. "Careful now."

He had warned her over and over again. The contract was made so that she could distinguish from emotions and plain labor. Was good sex considered labor? He did want an exclusive contract with her because he couldn't get enough of her in bed? She suddenly felt like a whore again. Whores were easily replaced. She hated the feeling, and for once, she was glad her parents weren't around to see her spiral into something as sad as this.

She had kidded herself about the friends with benefits plan. That could never happen. She was at a losing end. Just when she thought she had thawed his cold heart...

***

It had been two days since the tabloids released those photos and it had been two days since he had been feeling utterly miserable. He had meant for it to happen. He had meant for the media to see that. He couldn't bear to be in love with someone, the thought of actually loving Mikaela threatened his stability. He had spent an agonizing week, debating if he should end it to save his wits. In the end, his practicality won over and he sent her $20,000, hoping she would give up on him completely.

Justin had met Vida Karlovac a mere two days before he invited her to his home, something he had never done, all in an effort to forget about Mikaela. Vida was the poster girl for every other woman he had dated -- some degree of popularity, long legs, and an attractive face. But she was no Mikaela. The moment the photos exploded on media, his mother called him, asking him what happened between him and Mikaela.

He had insisted they weren't dating, but deep inside he wished he was. Like a normal couple would. He had gotten to know her better in London and it was something he had regretted. He wanted it to be a contract, plain and simple. All he had wanted was sex. The sex was mind-blowing, but her personality was out of this world.

He had never met anyone like her. It all started with that smile. Her smile brought his defenses down, something he hated to admit. It was why he tried to act as coldly around her as possible. He remembered seeing her for the first time across that room, and he told himself he had to get to know her. Her smile was radiant, just like her personality.

At first he thought it was only for the sex, and his reasons were selfish. He wanted her to himself entirely. No one was to have her. He didn't even want other men ogling at her or flirting. That was proven at the hotel. It was cute that she tried to make him like her, her efforts were messy and childish, but her intentions were clear. How can you fall in love in less than three months? He had made that contract so that he would know where his boundaries were, it wasn't just for her. Three months was pretty long, and he told himself he would tire of her in less than that time. He had wanted to use her body first; it was a physical attraction that led into something else.

He had become irrational over her. That contract was a first of many. He had told himself that friends with benefits wasn't in the books, and after sleeping with her three times, he knew he wanted her in a way he didn't want any other woman. She was the most beautiful person he had ever met, and he had met a lot of beautiful people. The only person on his mind was her. It took a while to acknowledge his feelings. It took a while to convince himself that he wasn't being silly. This was legitimate. He had fallen for her and he had ruined his chance to be with her, just to save his pride.

Time and time again, he told himself that he had to have someone perfect, if not perfect, someone close to his ideals. She didn't fit in any of those ideals, except that she was physically appealing and she had a sweet nature he also found in his family. That was it, right? There was nothing extraordinary about her. He told this to himself, there was nothing too unique about her that others didn't have… but he couldn't stop thinking about her.

He had debated that he was probably starved of affection and Mikaela was the closest thing to it. He had never been starved of affection before. He didn't like the feeling. It was as terrible as missing his father. He couldn't lack for love, he had all of that and more with his sisters and mother.

Since the day he had done the unthinkable, the harshest thing he could ever do to her, he couldn't sleep properly. Vida was game for everything, even readily stripping naked in the privacy of his pool, an open invitation to steamy sex. He declined, saying he had only wanted to get to know her better, and he thought they wouldn't make a good match for each other.

Luckily, Vida didn't throw a hissy fit.

"Your thoughts are with someone else," she said in a sexy Eastern European accent.

He could only nod. It was true. Only Mikaela filled his thoughts, night and day. Work was no escape. He couldn't stop thinking about her. He reasoned to himself he had acted on impulse, afraid of the growing emotions he wasn't used to. How could he deal with this? How could he kill of this emotion? Was he that afraid of commitment? He had made that contract so that she could stay committed to him, yet he couldn't do the same.

I didn't cheat on her, he told himself, *and I'm only breaking her heart.*

Only breaking her heart. His heart had never been broken. He was used to breaking hearts, but breaking Mikaela's heart made him feel remorse, something that had never happened before, too. Was it right to stick by his pride? It was what drove him to survive, it was what drove him to be successful.

Yet, here he was, feeling like a fool. A blundering idiot, feeling like he had made the worst mistake in the world. No matter how much he tried to rationalize, it still left him feeling jumbled up. There was only one way to appease his thoughts.

Moments later, he drove out, set on seeing her.

***

He walked into the coffee shop, telling himself everything was going to be all right, that she was going to see him, in fact he had prepared a spiel in his head. He walked with his head held high, with purpose in his stride.

"Is Mikaela here?"

"Mikaela? Who is that?" the barista began, looking blank.

Someone overheard him. Mary Ann came rushing to the counter. "You're looking for Mikaela?" she began. She had to get a good look at this man whom Mikaela was so giddy about. He was very handsome.

'Yes, Mikaela Johnson."

"She already left."

"You mean her shift ended?"

"No, she resigned. It was abrupt. A few days ago."

"Where is she?"

Mary Ann shrugged. "She didn't say much. But it looked like she had personal problems."

He should have called first. How stupid was he? He didn't even bother to ask if she was at the café. Such wasted time! He nodded and said his thanks, quickly dialing her number as soon as he got out of the coffee shop.

It rang and his heart pounded, wanting to hear her voice. It just kept ringing and ringing. *Answer. Answer. Come on. Please.* He dialed fifteen times, until an automated voice told him the line was out of coverage area. She could still be at the apartment. He raced to the apartment, glad he had the spare key with him.

He knocked first, breathless. There was no answer. He flung the door open and saw the apartment still intact with his furniture, all except hers. He ran to the bedroom, wishing against hope that she would be there. He had imagined this wrongly earlier. He had imagined she would go hysterical upon seeing him, and she would cry and ask why they couldn't be together, and he would forgive her for acting like every other woman he dated…

Her clothes were gone, there was no sign of her. The apartment had been stripped clean of her memory. He looked around wildly, wondering where she went. She couldn't have gone back to her old apartment, right? He was ready to reach for his phone, call the private investigator, when he heard a noise.

There was a small gasp and he spun around, seeing the one person that made his heart skip a beat. She was wearing a plain white shirt and jeans and sandals. The very look he used to dislike. Used to.

"What are you doing here?" Mikaela stammered, her eyes wide open, surprised he was here. Never had she thought she would see him again, that the last time she'd see him would be on a tabloid newspaper.

"I own this apartment," he stammered back. "I thought you left." Damn, that was a stupid thing to say.

"I forgot something," she replied, regaining her composure and walking past him without as much as a glance.

Justin saw her walk into the bedroom, rummaging for something in a cabinet. Moments later she walked out, and he was still rooted in the same spot. What was she looking for? He couldn't see it in her hands.

"I didn't tell you to leave the apartment yet," he uttered, not wanting her to leave his sight.

She spun around, moments before she could hold the door handle. There was a fire in her eyes he had never seen before. She was livid, and yet what made him uneasy was that she was quiet. She turned around again, determined to leave him.

"Did you hear what I said?" he said in a louder tone.

She faced him, walking up to him in slow, calculated steps. "I'm not part of your contract anymore. So you can foam at the mouth and command and demand all you want, but I'm not bound by you anymore. I'm glad you cheated on me. It showed me how much I was going to lose in the first place."

He looked confused. "What?"

"You heard me right. I'm not your plaything anymore."

"You were never my plaything," he replied. "I never thought of you as a toy."

"Then why did you do that to me?" she asked without flinching. *Yes, why would you? Why would you break my heart into a thousand pieces?*

Justin flinched when she asked that. Why did he? He had rehearsed this in his head. The reasons were ready to be spilled out. What were those again? He closed his eyes, trying to find the right words to say.

"I didn't mean to hurt you. I meant it, but I didn't mean it."

"Make up your mind," she snapped at him. "You're at it again, see? You make people feel like crap because you want to feel high and mighty. "

"It's true, my ego—"

"Is a hot air balloon," she finished for him. "You're the most selfish person I've ever met, I'm saying this again in case you forgot.

You're egotistical, you're an asshole, and you don't deserve the love and respect that you think you deserve."

That actually hurt, he thought. Women had said that to him before, but hearing Mikaela say that stung. He wasn't prepared for that.

"I know I don't deserve to be heard anymore, but please, just give me a chance."

"If you begged for this a few days ago, I would have."

"I had to think!"

"And you think I didn't have to think? I had to think for myself, I had to think about my survival. I had to think about my future after you cut the contract short, all for another woman."

"I thought about your future too. You couldn't have resigned without thinking it over--"— "

"Why? You think I can't get a job somewhere else? You think I'm dead without your money? I survived long enough without you and I can survive again without you."

"Where were you supposed to go?"

"Santa Monica, it's not far enough away from you, but I got the scholarship."

He was quiet for a moment. He knew she would get that scholarship.

"Take back your money. I don't want to be a part of it. I may need money, but I won't get it from you."

"No, I want you to keep it. I violated the contract, whether it was implied or not."

"Oh, implied? It was hell of implied, with your hand on her ass!"

"I didn't mean for it to end that way, but I was afraid—"

"Afraid of what, Justin? Afraid of losing your hard-earned money to someone like me? Afraid of losing your credible reputation as a playboy?"

"Afraid of falling in too deep with you," he interrupted her. "That was what I was afraid of. I didn't think this would happen. That contract was made to protect us both."

"It hasn't protected me," she cried out. "All it did was make me feel so bad, even if I deserved a shot at happiness. And I can't believe I imagined that with you." Her face reddened and that was when Justin knew it was the truth.

"For the record, it hasn't been easy, adjusting to your every whim. You think I was as crazy for the sex as you were? I did it for my future. And you know what makes me feel so bad? I felt like a whore, desperate to make ends meet—"

"I wanted to help you," he exploded. "I wanted you to finish college, I wanted to see you achieve your dreams. The moment we talked at the party, I knew there was something different about you."

"Why? 'Cause I was the most gullible person in the room?"

"I thought I saw the most beautiful person I had ever seen," he said. "I saw you, standing there alone, pretending you were waiting for someone. I suppose you were waiting for me and you didn't know it yet. I didn't either."

"Don't turn this into something romantic," she said bitterly. "I know where this is going. You think you're so frickin' charming—"

"Listen to me first."

"You never listen to me," Mikaela told him. "And frankly, I've had enough of this, I've had enough of all of this. You've trampled on me enough. I don't want to be a part of your mind games, I don't want my self-esteem affected, and I don't want to think twice before I talk because you might think less of me."

"I don't think less of you. I think the world of you. You're the most amazing person—"

"Stop it! Stop it!" she cried. "You're doing this on purpose. You think you can reel me back in, don't you? All those times I've tried to be nice to you, they fell on deaf ears, they fell on nothing. You looked at me like I was the lowest of the low, well-- guess what buddy, what you did was the lowest of the low."

"I only did that because I was afraid I couldn't control what was happening," he began. "I realized things when you were in London. I saw that look of happiness in your eyes and I wanted to keep it that way, but I didn't want to be obvious. And you're right, I have a huge ego. I wanted to come out as the winner of the contract, even if this was no contest, even if I told you this was a win-win situation.

"I wanted you, Mikaela, and I'm not afraid to say it. I wanted you from the moment I saw you. It started out with me just wanting to sleep with you. I'd lie to myself if I thought you weren't desirable, you were and I told myself if I didn't introduce myself to you, I'd regret it. I didn't want to get to know you at first, but I wanted you. It was selfish and I saw no other way to keep you close. I didn't think I'd end up liking you too soon. There was a reason that contract was only supposed to last three months, to avoid strong emotions.

"I'm not used to stuff like that. I'm not used to being nagged about, I'm not used to attention that borders on controlling. I dated long term, but I never fell in love. Maybe I felt some sentiment, some getting used to it, but that was it. Even a year isn't enough to make me love someone."

"It's not about the time! Time doesn't matter when you find yourself liking someone. Don't you want to spend every waking moment with someone you like at least?"

He nodded. "I realized that too late. I realized that this morning."

"So you came up with that plan? You did that on purpose, to make me feel bad. Do you have any idea how you made me feel? You did that for the whole world to see, when you knew you were only targeting me. Your hand on her butt, you were smiling on that photo—"

"Because I planned for it to be the like that. I gave you the money not because I cheated, but because I didn't want to see you again, knowing I'd have hurt you too much already—"

"Yet here you are."

"Yes, here I am," Justin told her, his eyes solely concentrated on her. "Here I am, asking for a chance to be with you, here I am bending down to pride. Here I am doing something I'd never done before. I was desperate to see you. I couldn't sleep.

Right after those paparazzi took those photos, I felt no sense of accomplishment. In fact, I felt miserable. You were on my mind every day, when you left London early, there wasn't an hour I didn't wish I could have taken that flight with you. It was a terrible last ditch effort to get rid of these feelings I'm not used to. I also get afraid, even if I'm like this, even if I'm used to making corporate decisions- this whole thing, it's all new to me."

"You're telling me this now? Do you think I'm a total idiot to even believe what you're saying? You could have said this while I was there!"

"I was a coward!" he exploded. "I was a goddamned coward. And I still am now. It took all of my strength, my pride, everything—just so I could garner that least amount of courage to see you. I had to see you."

"Why did you make things hard for me? Couldn't it have been easy to be nice at least?"

"I did all those things for you," he said. "The shopping, this apartment—"

"Only on loan," she cut him off. "Even your kindness was on loan. The moment you figured you'd tire of me."

"I haven't tired of you, that's why I'm here. I'm trying to explain the shitty stuff I did to you," he reasoned angrily.

She stopped. He had cursed, he had said the first profanity she had ever heard from his mouth. He saw her face and continued.

"So yes, I said shit, yes, I was an idiot for doing that to you, yes, it was lame I tried to protect myself from falling in love with you, but I couldn't."

Mikaela said nothing and waited for him to continue.

He took a deep breath, never breaking eye contact with her. "You heard me right, I fell in love with you, only I didn't recognize it earlier. The moment I did, fear was in place as well. The fear that I could never become who I molded myself to be, the fear that if I lost you, I'd feel so abandoned, I'd never allow myself to fall in love again. I prided myself in getting any woman I wanted, and I prided myself in getting you. I coerced you into signing that contract, I made you a part of the routine I'd always wanted to have. The sex was great and I wanted more of you because of that—"

"Is that why you didn't sleep with me that night? When we had our first real date? We spent hours talking and talking and I believed every word you said—"

"Every word I said was true. I couldn't bring myself to sleep with you that night because I wanted every waking moment with you to be real, far more real than that contract. I wanted to hear what you had to say, I wanted you to ask about me, so you could get to know me better."

"I already have. And you've hurt me so much it's enough to last me a lifetime," she told him, glancing at something on the table.

He picked the newspaper up. "Is this what's bothering you?"

She didn't say anything again. Everything about him bothered her.

"If this is, I told you, it was a stupid decision. I was selfish and only sought to protect myself."

"That's damn right, you're selfish."

"You have every right to be made at me, you have every right to send me away—"

"Take back your money. I didn't touch any of it."

"Money is a trivial thing."

"Of course it is for you! You know why I'm angry? I'm angry because I believed in you, I'm angry because I put so much hope into you, thinking you just might have that shred of real kindness in you for me—"

"It's there. You have all of me!" his voice rose. "I'm not the expressive type so this must be coming out wrong."

"You were wrong from day one. I shouldn't have ever allowed that first dinner. You were manipulative from the very start and I didn't see that—"

"I only wanted to keep you."

"Like an object? Like you owned me. I told you before, just because you've got that contract doesn't mean you own me. And you know what the worst thing is, I allowed it to happen. I lost my pride, I lost my freedom for you. I couldn't date other people because you didn't want me to, even if I only wanted you."

He remembered the flirting at the hotel and how he hated it. He didn't want anyone else near her. "So what if I'm selfish? I wanted you in my life, I still want you now."

"You think it's that easy to forgive you, huh?" Mikaela looked up with tears in her eyes. "You come back here, all dramatic, with a speech ready? And you think I'll be the same idiot I was five days ago?"

"I'm inclined to say yes but I know you'll take it against me. And you're not an idiot. I saw something in you. You stood out from the crowd. You in your blue dress and those heels. And that smile. Who could forget that smile? I didn't forget it the moment I saw it in the coffee shop. And you want to know another thing? I kissed you in your sleep."

"I know," she said, unable to control a few tears.

"You know?" he looked surprised.

She looked embarrassed but soldiered on. "I was looking at you while you were asleep. It was something that had never happened before, you actually sleeping beside me."

"I meant for that. I didn't want to leave right away." He remembered it well. He saw her lying there, and he couldn't resist the urge to leave without kissing her cheek at least.

"You wanted to stay?"

He nodded. "I allowed that to happen. I wasn't too afraid, maybe it was because it was just the two of us. No one else could see. But even if I allowed that, I still didn't want to seem vulnerable. Love isn't a weakness, but I've learned to keep away from it, except when its family. You -- you're the first person to do this to me. You screwed me over and you screwed me good."

Mikaela took a step back away from him. "Justin, I'm tired. I know it's been only two months and a week since this whole disaster, but I can't do this anymore. I'm too traumatized from this, from you. I humiliated myself, I did things I never thought I'd do, all because I wanted you to like me. I didn't expect it would go beyond that, I didn't expect I'd fall for you."

"It worked, Mikaela. Who wouldn't fall in love with you? Who wouldn't want to be with you? That smile alone snagged me. I tried to stay away, but no, I can't, I couldn't."

Her heart pounded, that same feeling she felt seeing him sleep beside her ever so soundly. That same feeling she felt when he smiled at her as she persistently asked questions.

Justin looked at her, knowing she was still debating about this whole scenario. "Mikaela, you make me feel like I'm on top of the world, like I've stepped up my game. When you left, Louisa called me. She dropped so many hints about you, it was clear they wanted you for me, and she was trying to tell me that. That I wanted you and I was in denial. I guess I'm an idiot for relying on practicality too much. There is not practicality when it comes to love, it was something I wasn't used to. I had wanted to be rational, but you make me irrational.

"I've known you less than three months, and you told me earlier it isn't about the time. You're right, it isn't. And it's strange to fall for you when I prided myself on never doing that. I guess there's a first for everything, and for that I'm glad."

She blinked and looked at him, her tears began to dry on her cheeks. "You are?"

"You were quite persistent," he smiled at her.

"I don't think I still will be."

"I'm asking for a chance."

"At what? Forgiveness?"

"A shot with you."

"I'm not for you. I'm no model, I'm not a millionaire. Do I look like I have a trust fund? I'm not a celebrity either. I'm just some barista with small time dreams."

"No dream is too small and I admire you for that. You know what my dream is? To get to date you, permanently date you. If you would allow me to. Why did you come back, anyway? Did you know I was going to be here?"

She shook her head. "I came back to get something."

"The apartment's been stripped clean."

She fished something out of her pocket. In her hand was the charm bracelet he got her, the first gift he had ever gotten her. She still kept it. He felt his heart leap. Was this a sign? But he didn't believe in signs. Although, now he suddenly wanted to. He felt desperate and it was a desperation that he had never had in his whole life. It was a desperation to be liked, to be loved.

He looked at her, not expecting much, but there was that little shred of hope left in him, a hope that she would reconsider him. *Would she?* He would practically grovel at her feet for her forgiveness at least…

"It won't work," she sighed.

His heart sank.

"I'm moving to Santa Monica and you'll be here."

The corners of his mouth curved and then he found himself laughing, a feeling he hadn't had in the last three years. He was actually laughing. And that was when he knew that she was the one.

"We'll figure something out. The important thing is that you finish school and that you're just an hour's drive away, or a fifteen-minute helicopter ride away."

"You'd really do that to visit me? Take a helicopter every day?"

"Or I could move there, buy a unit."

"You wouldn't."

"Try me."

"I already have," she said with an impish grin.

"Come here," he pulled her close to him, unable to believe this was really happening.

She smiled, surprised at this sudden display of affection. "I think I'm too close to you."

"I guess it's time to renew that contract," he murmured. "Something that borders on kissing in public, mandatory romantic dates and maybe a good old romp on whatever we get to lie on."

"I'm game for that," she replied, moving her face closer to him and tiptoeing.

"Good," he replied, near breathless. He looked at her and he was looking at the world. He would never let go of her, ever again.

Justin couldn't wait to kiss her every day, and he would start now.

THE END

Authors Personal Message:

Hey hey hey!

I really hope you enjoyed my novel and if you want to check out all my other releases then just head to my Amazon Page and see them all!

Remember

Peace, Love & High Heels

Lena x x

Fancy A FREE BWWM Romance Book??

Join the "**Romance Recommended**" Mailing list today and gain access to an exclusive **FREE** classic BWWM Romance book along with many others more to come. You will also be kept up to date on the best book deals in the future on the hottest new BWWM Romances.

* Get FREE Romance Books For Your Kindle & Other Cool giveaways

* Discover Exclusive Deals & Discounts Before Anyone Else!

* Be The FIRST To Know about Hot New Releases From Your Favorite Authors

Click The Link Below To Access This Now!

Oh Yes! Sign Me Up To Romance Recommended For FREE!

Already subscribed?
OK, Read On!

A MUST HAVE!

BABY SHOWER

10 BOOK PREGNANCY ROMANCE BOXSET

50% DISCOUNT!!

An amazing chance to own 10 complete books for one LOW price!

This package features some of the biggest selling authors from the world of Pregnancy Romance. They have collaborated to bring you this super-sized portion of love, sex and romance involving the drama of a baby on the way!

1 - Tasha Blue – The Best Man's Baby
2 - Alexis Gold – The Movie Star's Designer Baby
3 - Cherry Kay – The Tycoon's Convenient Baby
4 - CJ Howard – The Billionaire's Love Child
5 - Kimmy Love – Her Bosses Baby?
6 - Lacey Legend – The Billionaire's Unwanted Baby
7 - Lena Skye – A Baby Of Convenience
8 - Monica Castle – The Cowboy's Secret Baby
9 - Tasha Blue – Fireman's Baby
10 -Alexis Gold – The Billionaire's Secret Baby

START READING THIS NOW AT THE BELOW LINKS

Amazon.com > http://www.amazon.com/The-Baby-Shower-Pregnancy-Billionaires-ebook/dp/B01A5DEUP2

Amazon.co.uk > http://www.amazon.co.uk/The-Baby-Shower-

Pregnancy-Billionaires-ebook/dp/B01A5DEUP2

Amazon.ca > http://www.amazon.ca/The-Baby-Shower-Pregnancy-Billionaires-ebook/dp/B01A5DEUP2

Amazon.com.au > http://www.amazon.com.au/The-Baby-Shower-Pregnancy-Billionaires-ebook/dp/B01A5DEUP2

CPSIA information can be obtained
at www.ICGtesting.com
Printed in the USA
LVOW04s0409171116
513242LV00012BA/371/P